Angel ran. He ran fast. Somehow, he outran the officer again, and he stopped moving long enough to check in with Doyle.

There was no answer. Alarmed, he remotely played back his messages and heard what was obviously a veiled cry for help from Cordelia. Clearly someone had supplied her with a false name for Club Komodo, in order to throw off anyone who might hear the message. Doyle must have left the apartment to search for her.

I should have run after the limo, he thought, but he had to admit that he couldn't have caught up with it even if he hadn't stopped to talk to Meg. More likely he would have been hit by oncoming traffic or bullets or both, and taken to the hospital; and wouldn't that have been interesting when dawn came?

He was stymied.

Maybe even the Powers That Be can't deal with this one, he thought. *Maybe this is the one we can't even fight, much less win.*

And if that's true, more people besides that frightened little boy are going to get hurt.

Angel™

Angel: City of
Angel: Not Forgotten

Available from POCKET PULSE

ANGEL

not forgotten

An original novel based on the television series
created by Joss Whedon & David Greenwalt

Nancy Holder

POCKET PULSE

New York   London   Toronto   Sydney   Singapore

An *Original* Publication of POCKET BOOKS

 POCKET PULSE published by
Pocket Books, a division of Simon & Schuster Inc.
1230 Avenue of the Americas, New York, NY 10020

ISBN: 0-671-04145-2

First Pocket Pulse printing April 2000

10 9 8 7 6 5 4 3 2 1

POCKET PULSE and colophon are registered trademarks of Simon & Schuster Inc.

Printed in the U.S.A.

This one is most definitely for
Lara and April Koljonen.
You are my angels, and I love you both.

Acknowledgments

My deepest thanks to the cast and crew of *Angel*, especially Joss Whedon, David Greenwalt, David Boreanaz, Charisma Carpenter, Glenn Quinn, and Caroline Kallas. Also, to Debbie Olshan at Fox. From the bottom of my heart, thank you, Lisa Clancy, Micol Ostow, and Liz Shiflett at Pocket. To my agent, Howard Morhaim and his assistant, Lindsay Sagnette, you're both aces. For all their help and support, thanks so very much to Linda Lankford; C, as always; Karen Hackett and Sue Farley; and Jeff Mariotte and Maryelizabeth Hart.

PROLOGUE

Near Nias, in Indonesia, 1863

The dead hunted her.

She was cursed, and the cursed were their meat.

In the wind they chewed on her hair. In the rain they gnawed on her bones.

The dead were always starving.

As she crawled through the jungle, they sliced off her skin with their fanged teeth and drank her blood with the ends of their bony fingertips.

The spirits feasted on her living flesh. The delicious treasures, her organs, lay deeper. The most prized of these was her heart. With the cracked bones of their arms and legs, they gouged her in search of the delicacy.

The drums were the heartbeats of the dead, pounding faster as they closed in. The nearer she got to death, the louder the drums played. Soon the beats would catch the rhythm of her heart and change it. Like two sticks rubbing together, a spark would ignite. Then her heart would catch fire and burn her from the inside, until she was nothing but a pile of ash.

When her body was a memory, demon *jin* would rip her soul away and devour it. She would be damned to oblivion. She would not remember her life, or her self. Nothing of her would linger in the universe. She would simply be gone, forever.

Only Latura, God of the Dead, could save her from that fate now. The dead were in his thrall. If he commanded them to spare the cursed woman, they would.

And he would save her, because she alone knew the words that could grant him access to the world of men. Latura dwelled in the Underworld, with only demons and the dead for companions. His world was the closest thing to oblivion that existed. It was the stuff of hell.

It was hell itself.

Latura's twin brother, Lowalangi, was the god of the sky, the ruler of the heavens. Lowalangi had created the human race. Humans changed. They had adventures.

The dead never changed. They were static.

Latura yearned to surface from the underground

and dwell among the living. For this, he needed someone who would perform untold sacrifices, increasing the population of the dead so that he might take a rest from gathering their lifeless corpses.

Someone who lived, who would speak his name and perform unholy rites and rituals, concentrating magickal energy to strengthen him for the journey.

He must also have a vessel—a living body in which to dwell. It must be properly prepared, or it would burst into flame, and he would return to the depths.

The Servant understood now that her human lover had planned that fate for her. His betrayal had shocked her to her core.

Once he realized that she knew, he had professed his love for her, and told her he couldn't go through with her sacrifice. But she knew by then that that was a lie, too. He had foreseen his own death, and he must leave someone behind to carry on his work. If he did not, Latura would feed his soul to the dead.

So on pain of the same punishment, she became Latura's new acolyte. She had to learn the rites, and the incantations, and quickly, before her lover was found and killed. Or else Latura in his thwarted wrath would allow the *jin* to devour both their souls and grind them into forgotten dust.

3

Now her lover was dead, and she alone knew the words that would bring Latura forth. She was spared the "honor" of becoming his vessel. She was safe.

Unless the secrets of Latura were ever written down.

The Servant could not write. She had memorized everything by rote. That knowledge would keep her alive, at least until someone tortured the forbidden knowledge out of her.

Unless Latura lost his patience with her and gave her to the demons.

If she had known what it would be like to serve the god, she would never have begun the journey she now so bitterly regretted. The best she could hope for now was to escape the souleaters into the land of the afterlife. To exist as a phantom.

In misery, but to exist.

"Latura," she whispered. She murmured additional sounds, words that made no sense to her, were not a language of this time and this world. But they brought him forth, though only as an invisible power.

"Latura."

Lightning crackled. Wind roared through the jungle. Birds swarmed out, shrieking, as the trees swayed and fell.

"Latura."

4

The steamy jungle fell cold, unbelievably so; and a rotten stench rose like mist from the ground.

Panic spread through the jungle animals.

The drums fell silent.

She put her face to the ground and hid her gaze.

The earth shook; trees and ancient stones pitched with the sharp cresting of the jungle floor, rising, falling with awesome force as the God of the Dead walked the earth.

Fires flared up and made a ring around her. The world burst into flame. The moist jungle caught and began to burn. She felt the heat, smelled the smoke. She did not move.

The dread Lord of Shadows lifted her up. He carried her on his shoulders as she dragged herself through the tangles of vines and lush, primeval growth. Steam rose off the thick bamboo. Animals screamed. Some died. Snakes slithered.

Warriors in black jackets and crowns of feathers emerged shouting from the fiery landscape. Their spears sliced through stalks of bamboo as they advanced on her.

She was in Nias territory; the people were head-hunters and cannibals. Latura had commanded her to come to them, and promised that they would not take her head.

She trembled, hard. She was a Badui. Both sacred and outcast, Badui were forbidden to have contact with the outer world. They could not cut their hair. They could not eat four-legged animals. They could not touch money. They could not commit adultery, or steal.

For the sake of Latura, she had done many of those things.

The Badui woman, who called herself the Servant because her name belonged to another lifetime, had cut her hair to the center of her shoulder blades. She had loved a married man in secret, the Badui headman who had worshipped Latura. Her lover had been fierce, handsome, and terrifying. He had sacrificed to Latura in his name and her own, and they became Latura's devoted servants.

To this day, she didn't know how he had first contacted Latura from the depths. That secret had died with him. But before he had died, he had mingled his blood with her own, and passed the ability to commune with Latura to her. If she did not succeed in bringing the god into the world, it would be her duty to create a new Servant before she herself died.

Latura came to her, in the form of a whirlwind of fire, and told her many mysteries of life and death. He taught her incantations and secret potions. He could stop the progress of disease and decay. He promised to tell her the magick words that would spare her from death forever, if she would be faithful to him.

But in the three small forbidden villages of the Badui, it was impossible to keep secrets. Latura, the cruel and vicious God of Death, was a forbidden god. Before the Servant's human lover had been butchered by his own people, he begged her to escape while she had a chance.

The Badui villagers hunted her. But Latura protected her in return for her vow to go to Nias. First he called darkness, and the sky filled with lowering clouds. Then he called heat, and the jungles sizzled and steamed.

The villagers dogged her.

Latura sent a horde of demons. Hidden in the jungle, she watched as the green-skinned monsters ripped off the heads of her pursuers—many of them her relatives—and yanked their hearts out of their chests.

Those were the lucky ones.

For the others, death was more excruciating. Their hearts caught fire and burned inside their chests, igniting their blood until their bodies were burned to ashes.

Seeing this, the Servant trembled. She and her lover had given Latura their souls and she was his, forever. She would serve him to the end of days. Though her village had cursed her, her oath of loyalty was the stronger curse.

Now, as the headhunters converged on her, she

wept so hard that blood streamed from her eyes. Warriors whooped and called out to each other, racing at her with their spears held over their heads.

She prayed to gods who now shunned her.

Venice Beach, the present

"No one lives forever."
—Danny Elfman, Oingo Boingo

In the bright ocean sun, Meg Taruma sailed along on her in-line skates, listening to Oingo Boingo. The California-based group had disbanded a decade ago, and their leader, Danny Elfman, had since become a famous movie composer. Their macabre sense of humor and catchy rhythms were ageless, and she was sorry she'd never heard them live.

Six months into her new life, Meg lived in a funky old Victorian mansion in Venice Beach. Legend had it that a magician had owned the large shingled house with its bay windows and imposing turrets before it had been converted by his estate into apartments. At night the stairs creaked and wind whistled up the chimney flues. It was scary, but it was fun.

Kind of like Jusef, she told herself, and giggled.

Venice Beach itself was like every dream of southern California every Indonesian kid back home had: hip, crazy, sexy. Meg had felt at home as soon as Jusef had taken her there. She just knew it was where she had to live. And the Victorian building—called "Casombra"—was the only place they looked at before he signed a one-year lease for her.

For three months she studied voice and dance while he groomed her to be lead singer in his new band. In Asia, Jusef Rais was a huge rock star. But he wanted more. He wanted America. He was forming Bahasa Fusion around himself to achieve that. Meg firmly believed that he was going to be the next Ricky Martin, only Asian.

And she would be beside him all the way.

Jusef was the only son of an incredibly wealthy Indonesian family, the Raises. His father, Bang, was a cult figure in Indonesia. Bang was both idolized and feared, often by the same people. Thousands wanted him to lead the country, in whatever manner he chose: president, prime minister, dictator.

Jusef was intimidated in the extreme by his father, which Meg could understand. She'd rather do just about anything than be in the vicinity of Bang Rais. *Pak* Rais gave her the creeps. He was always watching her, always studying her. Jusef tried to laugh it off, tell her she was a hottie and could she blame the old man?

She never told Jusef that his father reminded her of all the men who had come and gone after the

9

death of her family. She wasn't sure he would understand. She and Jusef were both Indonesian, and they both knew she had asked for the treatment she had gotten by virtue of the path she had taken. Men were men. The woman who expected a man to be different from his nature was only asking for trouble.

But all that was just a shadow in an otherwise very sunny sky. Jusef had been afraid that his father would block his dream. As the only son, he was destined to take over the family empire. In Indonesia, sons must behave like sons. But Bang had indulged him and chose Jusef's cousin, Slamet, to be the next Rais to manage all their businesses.

Jusef moved to the family compound in Los Angeles to pursue his ambitions of American stardom. Slamet and Bang came over often, bringing along an entourage, and often stayed for months. According to Jusef, Bang's devoted followers were planning a government takeover.

Meg had no idea if that was so. At Jusef's order, she concentrated on her music. She exercised at the gym, took dance, and skated whenever she could. She had a sleek, athletic body now, and she dressed to show it off. She wore a pair of cutoff jean shorts and her baby tee was tight and seductive; she grinned when a few of the bodybuilders working out on the sparkling sand hooted at her. Her incredibly long, straight black hair was piled up on the back of her head, and it fell out of her hair clip as she picked up speed. She gave her hair a shake, and the steroid brigade applauded.

Her McDonald's bag was clutched in her right fist. She knew she was late for rehearsal. But Jusef would forgive her. After all, she was late because he'd kept her awake all night.

Talk about melting . . .

She giggled, feeling good, feeling young, feeling safe after all. She would never be Mary Margaret Taruma again, back in the killing fields, when every good thing in the world had been ripped to shreds.

She winced with physical pain at the threatening memories and pushed them away. She had worked on erasing them for over five years. Thanks to Jusef, they were almost gone.

She skated along, whistling Jusef's new composition. It was called "Raising the Dead," and she hoped it would be the hit that took them mainstream. Los Angeles was totally into "ethnicity," and their band, Bahasa Fusion, was primarily Indonesian. When over half the kids born in L.A. were non-Caucasian, there was a lot of room for stuff that reached beyond what Jusef called "the whitebread boundaries."

Jusef was tall for an Indonesian, with spiky black hair and those huge eyes that gazed into you forever and ever and ever. His chisled face and the large, brilliant flash of his smile were enough to make her do anything he wanted.

Oh, Meg, you've got it bad, she told herself.

But there was nothing bad about it.

Okay, a few shadows now and then. But she could deal.

"Hey, baby, what's happening, baby?"

It was the bow-legged old man who lived in an abandoned house a few blocks away. He wore a bright orange track suit and an old-fashioned hat with a long feather in it. He always waited for Meg against the chain-link fence. She brought him an Egg McMuffin every morning. He told people he had sung with Bo Diddley. He hadn't.

"Good morning," she said as she braked.

"Tingtang wallawalla bingbang," he replied. "I get it right?"

She chuckled. He had decided the nonsense phrase meant "Good morning" in Indonesian.

"Almost perfect," she assured him.

She handed him the McDonald's bag. Eagerly he looked inside for the Egg McMuffin and hot coffee. As far as she knew, it was the only real food he ate all day.

"You're a good girl," he told her, holding up the sandwich. *"Muchas gracias, amiga linglang."*

"You're very welcome." She smiled at him. "You take care of yourself."

"I knew Bo Diddley," he told her.

"Yes, I know."

"He used to bring me *two* Egg McMuffins," he added.

"I'll bring you two tomorrow, how's that?"

"Inky dinky parlez vous." He bit into the food with a blissful expression. *"A ramalama ding dong."*

"See you later."

"Chattanooga choo-choo. Do-wah-diddy-diddy."

She gave him a little wave and skated on. A few blocks on, she would run into Olive LaSimone, an elderly lady who claimed to have been a silent film star.

"Big as Mary Pickford," the old lady would say as she watered the geraniums in front of her apartment. She dyed her wisps of hair the same bright orange as the flowers.

Since there were no records of an actress named Olive LaSimone, she'd explain, "Pickford had me erased. She was jealous."

Jusef thought poor old Olive was funny. "She's like an ancient Egyptian," he'd told Meg just last night. "She thinks if she's remembered, she'll live forever. That's what all the people in Los Angeles believe. That's why they all want to be movie stars. If they're captured on film, they'll never die."

Meg had thought about pointing out that in a way, that was the truth. But it would sound too much like she was disagreeing with him.

Jusef didn't like that.

The ocean was blue, the air salty. She was young. There was no reason to anger Jusef or disturb the peace between them.

He had a temper, it was true.

Her skates were sleek and beautiful; she was almost flying off the ground, like a winged goddess. She passed the Dumpster, one of her landmarks, and hopped off the curb with a graceful leap.

She hurtled across the street, then up the driveway to the right, and around the corner. The apartment complex where Olive lived was next and—

Meg gaped at the smoking rubble where the building had stood.

And at the charred body on the sidewalk.

She screamed.

A blond woman, looking rumpled and tired in a khaki raincoat, flashed her a badge and said, "Please, move along."

But Meg froze. She stared, transfixed. She couldn't look away.

Olive's body was a black, melted ruin. Meg wouldn't have even known it was Olive, except for the few strands of bright orange hair clinging to the skull, and the tatters of Olive's brightly colored housecoat.

It didn't happen, she thought as old memories tried hard to surface. *It never happened.*

She began to shake.

The policewoman looked at her intently and said, "Did you know this woman? May I ask you a few questions?"

Beneath the bustling morning city of Los Angeles, Angel the vampire bolted awake.

Something's wrong, he thought.

CHAPTER ONE

Los Angeles, two weeks later

Flames geysered through the floor of the filthy apartment in East L.A. as Angel clutched at the enormous winged demon wrapped around his chest and neck. The monster snake hissed and writhed, so very eager to squeeze the life out of its intended victim. That being a totally useless effort, since Angel was already dead.

At least, technically.

The white-hot creature coiled tighter, burning a path through Angel's shoulders and upper torso. Good thing breathing was not an issue.

Too bad pain was.

Worse, I didn't bring marshmallows.

The apartment was an inferno. Towers of lottery tickets, racing forms, and foreign-language newspapers crackled and blazed as the shoddy furniture practically exploded in the heat.

Angel was appalled. *This is where the sweatshop bosses make their workers live. In fact, these are the good quarters. The ones you get if you exploit your own people.*

The rank-and-file workers existed in worse conditions than the average American prison inmate. In maximum security. In places where the prisoners rioted and killed guards because they were tired of living like animals.

With each flap of the serpent's large leathery black wings, the flames rose higher. A lamp with a red silk-fringed shade went up like a torch. Hordes of panicked rats scurried through the debris. One rodent burst into a writhing ball of flame, then fell through the rickety, burning floor and disappeared.

Atop a crate of charred sewing machine parts, a hand-painted fan decorated with green-faced demons and a shriveled-up Styrofoam bowl from Rice King vanished, incinerated.

As Angel battled the monster, a tall male figure appeared in the doorway. Angel had the sense that he had simply materialized, like a ghost. Though his features were obscured by the flames, Angel could see his silhouette in tight black clothing. The man said nothing, did nothing. He simply watched.

As Angel managed to get his hands around the

snake's thick body again, the man gave his fingers a snap. The snake's hide became as rough as shards of broken glass, piercing Angel's palms and fingertips. With a sharp hiss, the snake lunged, fresh, evil intelligence in its gaze. Its black tongue flicked as it struggled to sink its fangs into his face.

"Your workers are going to burn to death!" Angel shouted.

The man made two fists, then extended his arms and stuck out his thumbs. From his knuckles, blue flames crackled and hurled across the tiny room.

Without a moment's hesitation Angel released the snake's head and tucked in his chin. He kept his eyes closed against the ultrabrilliant intensity of the magickal energy as he grabbed at the snake's thick coils and hefted them into the path of the energy burst.

Seconds before it was hit, the snake sank its needle-sharp fangs into the crown of his head. Then it shrieked in agony and let go of him as the blue energy penetrated its body. Angel managed another successful block with the creature's convulsing body as the man tried one more time to strike him.

Pieces of the snake thudded to the floor. Angel dropped the rest, successfully dodging another barrage of blue flame erupting from the stranger's hands. Crouched tight and low, he rolled to the right, seeking protection behind a dressmaker's form.

The man muttered in a language he didn't know, and a phalanx of wicked-sharp, curved knives screeched through the air like heat-seeking missiles. They struck the dressmaker's form. From the cuts, blood gushed. The blood reeked and smoked.

The man moved his hands again, giving form to whatever he was going to launch at Angel next.

It was not one, not two, but three winged serpents.

Angel yanked two of the knives from the dressmaker's form and held them up and out, impaling two of the creatures. They screamed, wriggling like eels on fishhooks. Angel deftly flung them into the flames, where they exploded in showers of not-tempting bite-sized pieces. The third, still intact, sailed over Angel's head.

The man clapped his hands. A human skull formed between them. The skull bulleted directly at Angel, coal eyes glowing, teeth clacking.

Angel lunged at the skull and grabbed it with both hands, then slammed it against the floor. It shrieked like a dusted vamp, and exploded just like a dusted vamp. Into, well, dust.

The third serpent took that moment to charge him again. This time, it dropped to the overheated floor and wriggled toward Angel, moving with lightning speed. Angel timed his leap into the air; the serpent flew upward after him, but Angel landed well behind it. His boot heels crunched through the burning floorboards and he purposefully landed on his back, out of the way of the weakened area.

The serpent fell through the newly created gap in the floor. Then it exploded, sending a shower of half-cooked meat everywhere, including on the sleeve of Angel's black leather duster.

"Hey," the vampire protested.

Across the room, the stranger's hair began to smoke. Light flared around him; by his features, he was Asian, possibly Malaysian. His brows were heavy over eyes like black holes. His nose was hooked, his chin square and jutting.

Thick, black smoke poured from his nose and eye sockets. He raised a hand and pointed at Angel. His eyes, encased in blistering flesh, gleamed scarlet, blank and dead.

"You," he said, though his lips didn't move, "half-living. This world does not want you. You will never be safe. You will die alone, and forgotten.

"My god will eat your soul."

The room whipped into a firestorm. A rushing whirlwind of fire vortexed around Angel, surrounding him. The room became nothing but a smoky blur of orange and red. Tendrils shot out at him, grabbing for him like fingers. They ripped at his clothes, his hair, his face.

The bottom of his duster burst into flame, and he

beat it out with his hands. His skin began to blister. Even his eyes got hot.

Then the fire turned blue. Everything in the room was tinted the same crackling, intense hue as the energy the tall man had sent out.

The blue flared, then hardened. It froze. Ice formed. Where flames had danced, icicles crackled and glittered. Frost formed on the windows and the piles of dead rats.

Inside the fire, where the man had stood, the figure of a lovely, slender woman materialized. She could be no older than nineteen or twenty. Her blue-black hair bobbed around her head, as if she danced under rushing, turbulent water. Leaves and flower petals of gold threaded through her hair glanced and glistened.

She was dressed in a tunic of gold cloth so shiny it gave off a supernatural brilliance. Scores of gold bangles shimmered as she waved her curved hands very slowly. Tapered golden fingernails extended several inches from her hands. Leggings of darker gold molded her firm thighs. Her knees were bent and her feet tightly flexed as she dipped and bowed.

Angel thought of Siamese shadow puppets, their ornate decorative surfaces invisible to their enraptured audiences, who watched their mythic performances for ten, twelve hours without a break. Of exotic lands where saffron-robed men lost themselves in meditation and ritual. He heard temple bells, gongs, the rhythmic pounding of bamboo on stone, and the sweet, clear soprano of a young girl.

He had been to such places. Lived in such places.

Slowly she lifted one leg behind herself, tilting her head as she struck a pose. Shifting her weight ever so slightly, she began to inscribe a circle in the world of blue ice.

As she turned, she saw him.

She stopped dancing.

Tears coursed down her face. She opened her mouth and formed words he couldn't hear but nevertheless understood: *Help me*.

Slowly the blue ice melted away. The room looked like an underwater wreck. Where flames had risen to the ceiling, now there were only piles of ash and misshapen hulks that had been pieces of furniture. A blackened painting of a lush, mountainous landscape slid off the wall, scattering charcoal remnants of wooden boxes and crates.

A rat, its back smoking, skittered over Angel's shoe and disappeared.

Of the beautiful girl, there was no sign. Nor any of the magick-wielding stranger.

Then he heard distant screaming, drowned out in seconds by the wild shrieks of ambulance and fire-engine sirens.

The sound of his movements masked by the din,

he slogged through the room and barreled through the crumbling doorway. He flew up the stairs, taking them two, three at a time, expecting at any moment that they would give way.

They didn't. He reached the landing and ran to the nearest door. It was black and smoking, like the walls around it. There was sobbing and pounding behind it. The knob was white hot.

Behind him, the stairway collapsed with a roar like a huge, dying demon. The sobbing became screams of terror.

"It's okay!" Angel bellowed, straining to be heard.

He put his shoulder against the door and pushed steadily. The boards bowed but did not give way. He pulled back, then rammed, hard.

The wood cracked and splintered. Smoke streamed out, catching him unawares. He coughed and took a step backward.

A hand shot through one of the splits and reached wildly, grabbing at Angel's pants leg.

"Help us!" came a frantic plea. The voice was that of a young woman.

"Angel?" a second female voice yelled. It was Nira Surayanto, his client, who had called him for help. She was the reason he had come here tonight.

"Nira?" he called.

"Get us out of here! We can't breathe!" Nira broke into a fit of coughing.

"Stand away from the door," Angel ordered.

He rammed harder and burst through. The room was completely filled with smoke.

He squinted through the haze. A hand clasped his. Then he was surrounded by at least half a dozen young women, none older than eighteen, and a gaggle of children. They were grabbing at him, shrieking like they were drowning.

Moving swiftly, he led everyone into the hall. Nira was the one holding his hand. She was around eighteen, short and thin, her hair black and cut along her jawline. Her jeans and orange boatnecked T-shirt were covered with soot.

As she gazed up at him, her fingernails dug into his palm. She burst into tears. Two of the other women joined in. Then Nira wiped her eyes and spoke resolutely to the others, and all of them forced themselves to be calm. The tears mingled with soot had turned their faces into monstrous masks.

"Nira, is there a fire in there?" Angel asked, holding her shoulders and peering into her face. The smoke was thick and oily, billowing around them as it poured from the room.

"Yes."

"Is everyone accounted for?"

"Yes, *pak*," she told him, surveying the group.

"Come on," he urged, mindful that their escape route in the front of the building was cut off.

Just then a group of firefighters burst through the front door. One of them stared up at Angel and said, "Don't move! The floor's about to go. Man, we got here just in time."

Nira asked Angel, "Do you believe in miracles?"

The centuries-old vampire replied, "Something like that."

The firefighters brought in a tall ladder and leaned it against the shuddering upper floor. They raced to help the women down before the creaking ceiling gave way.

The fire captain ordered Angel to leave, but he pointed out—reasonably, he thought—that he was already standing on the unstable surface. There was no sense risking sending the survivors crashing through the floor by his moving off the platform just so another person could take his place. The captain retorted that a gas leak was likely, in which case the entire building was going to go up.

"Your family would sue the dickens out of us if you went up with it," she concluded.

"I don't have a family," he said flatly. "And I'm not going anywhere."

Maybe she realized it was useless to argue with him. She gave him a nod and snapped, "You guys, move your butts. This civvie goes up, someone besides me is going down."

*   *   *

They worked together, the captain giving orders to the firefighters while Angel supervised the survivors. Two of them succumbed to smoke inhalation and had to be carried down the ladder on stretchers. One little girl was badly burned on the back. Her eyes were clenched in pain, although not once did she cry out. Angel would have felt a lot better if she hadn't remained so rigid and composed. Better to get the fear and horror out of her system. Purge. Only then could the healing begin.

As Nira was taken to an ambulance, he walked beside her gurney and said, "I'll be by later tonight. I'm going to need your help to shut these people down."

She pulled her oxygen mask from her face. "No," she breathed. "You got me out. That's all I asked you for." She coughed. Her voice was hoarse. "I'll pay you as soon as I get back from the hospital. I've got some extra money stashed, for back home, and—"

"Not an issue," he told her firmly. "But this isn't over, Nira."

"But—"

"Help me stop this from happening to someone else," he said. He had no idea if she knew about the use of magick. And he didn't want to talk about it with onlookers.

"They almost killed me," she croaked. "That

27

man . . . a man came upstairs after I phoned you. He said we'd make great sacrifices."

"Miss, please keep your mask on," said one of the paramedics.

Nira did as she was told.

Her huge eyes stayed on Angel as they loaded her into the ambulance. He watched it pull away, slowly, the driver dodging the crowd that had formed. Slack-eyed druggies, wide-eyed children. Women from the neighborhood, making the sign of the cross, causing him more mental discomfort than anything else.

Angel had no clear sense of how long it took to get the scene locked down. That happened to vampires sometime. One lived so long that sometimes hours flew by like minutes. Other times a few minutes could telescope into a lifetime—

"Question: Do you always ignore police officers, or just the ones you know?"

Angel blinked. Detective Kate Lockley was facing him. Her blond hair was twisted in a makeshift coil, and she wore a khaki raincoat. No makeup, but she looked equally beautiful with or without it. She held an umbrella. He glanced up at the night sky, surprised. It was raining, and he hadn't even felt it, hadn't noticed it.

"Just the ones I know," he told her.

She sighed. "I asked you what you were doing here."

"Living *la vida loca.*" He didn't want to test her goodwill—such as it was—so he added, "One of the survivors is a client. She wanted out. Apparently the ringleaders enticed girls—Asian immigrants—with promises of teaching them English and giving them decent jobs. Then they used them for cheap labor. Sewing mostly. Or farmed them out to other rich Asians as maids and waitresses."

"And hookers?" Kate asked sharply. "Was your client working as a prostitute?"

Angel shrugged. "I don't think that word came up."

"Did the initials I.N.S.? Are these women in this country illegally?"

He frowned at her. "Kate, lighten up. They almost died in that fire."

"I can't look the other way just because they've had a hard day, Angel," she said, her blue eyes flashing. "We have laws in this country. Which, it may surprise you to know, help prevent situations like this one."

"You're right. It may surprise me." He turned to go.

"Hey." Her irritation level rose. "Don't go all self-righteous on me. My job is to protect and serve."

Angel ran a hand through his hair. He was tired. He was filthy.

And it was almost dawn.

"I won't kid you that I think our immigration policy is just or fair," she said. "But it's the policy we have. Complete with laws to enforce it. These people want better lives, but they automatically victimize themselves and their children by getting into this country illegally."

"All some of 'these people' want is any kind of life," Angel replied. "Freedom from starvation. Or political persecution."

"You running for office?" she snapped.

They regarded each other. She was the first to sigh. Maybe she was too tired to spar. She didn't usually give up so easily.

"I'll get her name from the hospital if you don't give it to me," Kate said, more gently.

"Nira Surayanto. She called because her 'supervisor' was threatening her. Apparently he tried to kill her tonight." He wished he'd had longer to talk to Nira. "She put a lot on the line to call me."

"I'm glad she did," she said simply. "But could you, just once, give *me* a call and let me in on the action? Let me know when something's going down? It *is* my job, you know."

"All right, Commissioner Gordon."

She smiled at the Batman reference. "I look pretty stupid when you get to all my crime scenes first."

"You never look stupid, Kate." He was sincere.

She sighed and combed her fingers through her hair just as he had, perhaps unconsciously. "What's your deal, Angel? What are you really doing in Los Angeles?"

"Looking for that big break," he said. *Old questions, old dodges.*

She waved him off. "You have the right to go home and clean up before you come down to make your statement."

"Tonight," he said. "I'll come down, and I'll be chatty. But right now I'm beat. Give me the day."

She frowned. "That's a long time to wait for an eyewitness account."

"The fire was going when I got here," he said.

"There was a body," she said flatly. "In fact, strange as it may sound, I think it might have started the fire."

He looked at her.

She huffed. Kate was not one to share much. "Look, I've got some strange homicides I think may trace back to this charming situation."

"Oh?" He raised his eyebrows.

She shook her head. "Way I see it, you don't need to get involved."

"Unless someone asks me to get involved."

"It won't be me." Kate's voice was firm. "And if anyone else asks you to, I expect to be notified."

Angel gave her a tired salute and walked into the shadows.

Not on your life, he thought.

Generally, for one reason or another, the people Angel helped couldn't go to the police. The helpless, Cordelia called them. Angel was their last hope.

And they were his.

He looked over his shoulder. Kate was scowling after him, frustrated. Then she stepped around the sawhorses draped with yellow police tape and began directing beat cops while she talked to the fire captain. Her phone went off, and she took the call. A million things at once.

Business as usual.

The sun was on its way; he could feel its power even in the predawn darkness.

Doyle would be staggering home from the clubs. Cordelia would be asleep, dreaming of fame and fortune. As he recalled, she had an audition today.

It's just another magic Tuesday, he thought as he climbed into his convertible and started the engine. *Talk about a rut.*

I need a hobby.

Or a vacation.

But Angel, the only vampire in existence possessed of his human soul, was in line for neither. He had arrived in Los Angeles seeking peace, hoping for sanctuary from his love for Buffy Summers, the Vampire Slayer. He had yet to find it.

He drove the streets. He pulled his car into the

covered parking lot and strode into his building. He needed to get inside. The sun was close to rising.

He unlocked the door to his office, crossed the threshold, and shut the door after himself. Quickly he scanned the interior—the well-worn sofa, the desks and chairs, reminding him of an old thirties' *noir* detective movie.

The message machine was blinking. The image of the golden woman flashed through his mind as he quickly crossed to the machine. He pressed the 'Play' button.

"Um," murmured a feminine voice, "I need help. I—"

On the tape a dial tone sounded. The caller had quickly hung up.

Or been disconnected by someone else.

Angel dialed *69, only to be informed by a flat computer voice that it was not possible to use the redial feature with the number.

Cell phone, he guessed. Whoever she was, he hoped she called back soon.

If she can.

CHAPTER TWO

In the last traces of night

Deep below the compound, in the temple Jusef Rais had built to Latura, a young girl named Julie Gonda cried out and fell to the floor as he grabbed her cell phone and smashed it against the cement.

"Who did you call?" Jusef demanded.

She buried her face in her hands. He heard her quiet sobs.

She knows I hold the power of life and death over her. There is nobody in her world stronger than I. I am her god. He grabbed her hair and yanked her head back, forcing him to look up at her. The terror on her face was the most powerful aphrodisiac in the universe. He wanted her. But he would leave her untouched. She would be a more fitting sacrifice for Latura.

Latura. He didn't even know what his god looked like. From the bits and pieces he, his father, and his cousin, Slamet, had gathered over the years, he had tried to build a temple that would please the Lord of the Dead. He must have succeeded at some level, for the god continued to favor them.

More specifically, to favor me, he thought, pleased.

Finally she rasped, "He told me . . . he . . ." She trailed off, as if she realized she had said far too much.

"Decha? Decha Sucharitkul?" he queried.

She gasped.

He ground the heel of his shoe into the fragments of her cell phone, at the same time realizing that he should have left it intact. It would have been a lot easier to find out who she'd called. And how she had managed to get it to work underground.

Well, I can torture it out of her pretty easily.

"You traitors, with your pagers and your cell phones and your 'lookouts.' You're really pathetic."

He yanked harder. She screamed as a huge chunk of hair was ripped from her scalp. To silence her, he kneed her in the chest. She began to cough.

"Decha told you I was with him, didn't he? He snuck into a room and made the call. Told you it was safe to sneak in here and defile my temple?"

"It was built defiled," she said bravely.

He considered that. "True."

He and the others had built the temple as best

they could. Their information had been very spotty, so they had improvised. They assumed that the God of Death demanded images of death in his holy places. They had done their best to please: The walls were painted with murals of mass tortures, executions, and the heaps of dead caused by disasters and plagues. Piles of skulls, both human and animal, lined the walls like bookcases, with prayers to Latura stuffed into the jagged mouths. Candles gleamed in the eye sockets.

Atop the skulls lay written spells, or *mandi*, written on bamboo rods and pages made from bark, as in the old days. They were prayers of supplication for protection, for revenge, and to aid in the quest of finding Latura's Book. The blood of their victims had been sprinkled over the spells to transform the words from thoughts into being. For as it was said in many religions, *The blood is the life*.

Buckets of blood were stacked in the four corners of the temple, which had, itself, been carved from living rock. The original builders of the compound—which dated from the twenties—had not used the subterranean spaces at all. The realtor who had sold the three-acre compound to Jusef's family had been told that the caverns were originally created in order to house bootleg liquor. But that plan had not been put into effect, and they had sat idle all this time.

After some debate Jusef had succeeded in convincing the others not to use electric lighting in the temple. In the ancient days Latura had felt closest to the cannibalistic headhunters of Nias, and the people had burned torches for their heat and light. Fire was a god to them. And so fire would light Latura's new temple.

Soot scorched the fantastic ceiling, which was carved by Indonesian artisans to resemble a rib cage. The individual ribs stretched from behind the stacks of skulls to the top of the tall room.

The sacrificial altar itself was the literal heart of the room. Likewise carved from stone, it was coated with metal—Jusef's single concession to the changes time had wrought in Latura's legacy. When victims were made to burn on it, the metal increased their agony. Agony was important to Latura. Pain and terror were the only sensations available to him in the Underworld, for they belonged to the damned and dying.

A likeness of Latura, demon god of shadow, embraced the altar. Again, working from vague references, Jusef and the others aimed for correctness in depicting their master, but had no idea how close they had come. In the jungles of Java they had listened to recited accounts of the First Servant, passed from generation to generation in song and dance.

Based on those tales, they had carved in stone what they believed Latura looked like: His face was a nightmare of slashes, wounds, and a huge, gaping maw. His gigantic head and huge, glowing eyes towered over his thirteen arms, covered with spines made of sharp stainless-steel knives. Jusef never washed the knives. Layers of blood had thickened, hardened, and grown moldy. The lesson: Beneath the decay exists that which does not rust.

Life eternal.

More spines covered his bent legs, of which there were seven, ending in webbed, taloned masses of stone. He had a forked tail, and his wings were huge. They enfolded the altar in jealous possession.

Maggots and other bugs skittered night and day over the stone and metal. Jusef knew they had sacrificed over two hundred people on this very altar, and many more back in Indonesia.

But the Gonda chick had begun to undo some of the work: She had begun the Rite of Cleansing, which Jusef didn't know. Left of the altar there was a clean spot, devoid of the unholy power of Latura. That meant that she had been successful in her magickal efforts, as far as she had gotten. So either the opposition had learned more scattered bits of knowledge about Latura than he and his family, or they actually possessed the Book. That notion was almost too painful to entertain, but as his father always said, *Prepare for the worst, and hope for the best.*

Either way, he would know everything this girl knew before she died on the altar.

"Resuming," he said calmly. "I assume you called our friend Decha some time ago to make sure the coast was clear. Did you call him back just now to let him know you'd gotten in here?"

She nodded. "Yes."

"Liar!" he flung at her.

"I'm telling you the truth," she insisted. Her voice quavered. "Please, *Pak* Rais, believe me."

He grabbed her by her hair again and started dragging her across the stone floor.

"He's dead," he said calmly. "He's been dead for hours. After he refused to tell me anything useful, I set his heart on fire."

Though tears welled in her eyes, she kept her face a mask. He was impressed by her courage.

He said, "You can't talk to dead people, no matter how powerful your cell phone."

She smiled—actually smiled—at him.

"You're right," she said.

She began to gag. He watched, perplexed. Blood and spittle foamed over her lips.

"No!" he screamed.

She smiled once more.

Blood spurted from her mouth like a geyser,

spraying him. A wave of blood smacked him in the face and dripped down his chin as her body flailed in violent convulsions.

"Stop it, stop!" he cried.

There was a mixture of triumph and sadness in her face. Then she went limp. Her eyes lost their focus.

She was dead.

"Latura, eat her soul!" he shrieked, livid. In his rage, spittle flew from his own mouth.

He threw the body down and stood. Facing his god, he made two fists and shook them.

"Latura, drag her down into hell with you!"

"It's a little late for that," said a voice in the darkness. Jusef turned.

A blue pinpoint of light hovered in the blackness of the cavern. It grew, and spun. It gained size as well as speed.

His father appeared, surrounded in blue energy.

"Father?" he asked, stunned. "How . . . what was that? Are you a spirit?"

"So you wish," Bang Rais said. "You have no idea what I'm capable of, Jusef." He narrowed his eyes. "But I've had a pretty good idea of what you're capable of. For some time."

The blue glow dissipated. Bang Rais, one of the most feared men in Asia, regarded his son with contempt.

"You thought you would cheat me," he said. "You thought you would lie to me."

He took a menacing step toward his son. "You also thought I was in Dakarta. That I had no idea that you have been trying to defraud me out of my chance for immortality."

"No, Father," Jusef said, backing away. "If you've heard anything, it's wrong. It's my enemies, trying to cause problems between us."

His father shook his head. "Don't try to save yourself. You killed Decha Sucharitkul trying to learn the location of the Book. When the apartment caught on fire, you had no thought of consequences."

"It didn't seem as if there were any," Jusef said weakly.

His father narrowed his eyes. "But what you didn't know was there were girls there, locked upstairs by one of our sweatshop supervisors, because he wanted them to become prostitutes. One of them had already called the outside for help.

"That help arrived. In time. But she didn't call a man, my son. She called a demon."

Bang Rais stared at his son. "It was a demon I failed to kill. Now he will follow the trail you've left."

"Who? What kind of demon?"

"No one you need concern yourself with. Since you'll be dead."

Jusef held up his hands. "Father, no. You misunderstand."

His father walked toward him. He was tall and muscular. But he was also tired. The magickal means—unknown to Jusef—that his father had employed to transport himself into the temple had exhausted him.

This is my only chance to save myself, Jusef thought desperately. *But how can I? I don't know the magick my father does. I don't even know how that Gonda girl got her phone to work in here.*

That girl . . . Jusef was seized with sudden inspiration.

The cleansing.

He walked toward his father and said, "Father, aren't you feeling well?"

Then he grabbed Bang Rais, who towered over him, and flung him into the spot Julie Gonda had sanctified. It had been said—but never tested—that Latura would abandon anyone who walked on holy ground. Jusef crossed his fingers that the god would consider a cleansed portion of his own temple holy.

His father was startled. "What are you doing?"

Taking care to remain out of the cleansed area, Jusef pulled out a talisman and held it before himself. It was a miniature version of the Mark of Latura: a fiery heart set within the mouth of a demon skull.

"God of Mystery, stop his heart," he chanted. "Stop the beat. Stop the blood."

"Jusef!" his father roared at him. "Stop this!"

"Stop him," Jusef continued. "He is a clean thing. He is a thing of goodness. Feel his goodness, and destroy it."

"No!"

Bang lumbered toward him. Then he cried out, clutched his chest, and fell forward. His face made a hard smack against the concrete. Blood pooled out.

He lay facedown and didn't move.

Warily Jusef watched him. He watched him for at least half an hour.

Then, satisfied that his father was dead, Bang Rais's only son began to laugh so hard he cried.

Later that morning

Meg was still sobbing when Jusef came into the Venice Beach dance studio not far from her apartment. Jusef rented the place for band practice when there were no dance classes. Guitars, percussion instruments, and a drum kit took up some of the space. The rest was taken by the traditional instruments of the ancient gamelan music of Bali: the ugal, a xylophone-like instrument; gong chimes, drums, cymbals, and *gangsa,* played with hammers.

Jusef had recently showered, and he smelled of

sandalwood soap and coconut shampoo. He was wearing black jeans, cowboy boots, and a black T-shirt. Despite her meltdown, she was stirred by the sight of him. The word *honey* came to mind, in all the languages she was fluent in: Bahasa Indonesia, English, her native Javanese dialect, and Dutch.

"Meg, what's wrong?" he asked, filled with concern. He crouched down beside her chair. The rest of the band had gone out back to smoke, giving her some privacy.

"There was another burning," she said. In the two weeks since Olive's death, there had been three more like hers. "It was on the news."

"And it's hitting too close to home," he said. She nodded.

"Did the police call you this time?" he asked. They had, the other two times, only because she knew Olive. So they said. But she wondered if they knew about her past.

"No. But that same detective, that woman who talked to me, was on the news. Detective Lockley."

"Do they have any leads?" he asked, caressing her shoulders. She rested against him, feeling the muscles in his chest pressing on her cheekbone. No one on earth was as strong and powerful as Jusef. No one would ever take as good care of her.

"They didn't say. It was at an apartment building in the garment district. They said people were living there and the conditions were terrible. Some man owns it and he said he didn't know what it was being used for. He just rented it out."

"The police didn't call," he repeated.

She shook her head. "Why should they?"

He shrugged. "I don't know." He laughed and ran a hand through his hair. It was incredibly silky and full. His eyelashes were long; they brushed against her skin as he pressed his forehead against hers.

"They said it might be necklacing," she continued, in a hushed voice. "That's something they do in Africa."

"Also, it's a form of execution in organized crime," Jusef said. "Gangs and *tongs* do it here in the States. It's a painful way to die, so I'm told."

She shivered. "When I was growing up, I always heard that America was a violent place. I had no idea."

He sighed. "I shouldn't have brought you here."

She warmed, hearing the self-recrimination in his voice. "But Indonesia is dangerous, too."

"If my father ran things over there, it would be safe to walk alone at one, two in the morning," Jusef said fiercely. "The world's going to hell, Meg. It's up to people like my father to save it."

By taking away everyone's freedom. Imprisoning anyone who dares to criticize the great Bang Rais, she thought. But she kept her own counsel.

"I will keep you safe," Jusef said to her. He lifted her hand to his soft mouth and kissed her knuckles. "You're very precious to me. There's no one else like you in the entire world."

"The way you say it, I almost believe you," she murmured, wanting more reassurance.

"It's true. I know it for a fact." He smiled at her. "You're unique. Irreplaceable."

She wrinkled her nose, letting go of the bad memories, as he had taught her, concentrating on him instead.

"You make me sound like a Ming vase," she accused him playfully.

"Or some other kind of precious vessel," he replied. He stood and pulled her to her feet. "Ready to get to work?"

She nodded.

"That's my Meg. I'll call the others back in." He pulled a cigarette from a pack on a yellow three-legged stool. "Take a moment. Wash your face."

Jusef crossed the room to the back door, where the others were smoking.

Meg looked at herself in the mirror.

"God, I look like death," she muttered.

Then she went to wash her face.

CHAPTER THREE

Later that afternoon

"My breath is so fresh," Cordelia Chase trilled as she clomped up the stairs of the Cooper Building. She was in the garment district, smack in the middle of downtown Los Angeles, and she wasn't there because it was fun to hunt for bargains. Winding her way among dingy brick buildings missing half their windowpanes and trying on clothes in places where the only dressing room was a blanket thrown over a rope had never been high on her list of "oh yay."

In the old days I never even looked at a price tag, she thought mournfully. *Now all I do is worry about money.*

It was a dry and blistering afternoon. It had been a long day, not made any easier by Angel. Just as she'd been getting ready for her audition this morning, he had called and asked her to check the machine throughout the day while he slept. Something about a fire last night, and a hangup phone call, and that it was very important to return any calls from some girl named Nira. No reason why, of course.

Maybe Nira equals he's over Buffy, Cordelia thought, surveying the mob scene in the first store on her right. *It's only been a couple months here in L.A. but hey,* he *was the one who broke up with* her.

Despite the proliferation of outlet stores, the L.A. garment district was still famous. Still a bargain-hunter's paradise, too, for Armani and Hugo Boss and all kinds of yummy labels. Tour buses dislodged shoppers from as far away as Las Vegas.

Hope the trip's worth it. For them and for me.

Hope Nira calls, if that's what he wants.

She'd had to monitor the phone because he was exhausted. He told her he hadn't been sleeping well, and really needed to catch up. *Like what, if he doesn't get enough sleep he'll die or something?*

So, maybe not *over the thing with Buffy after all.*

To be nice and, well, okay, job, she'd agreed to keep checking for calls. But that *so* wreaked havoc with her preparation for her audition. However, that was business as usual when you worked for a super-hero.

She frowned as she looked around at all the other

women and girls, bags of bargains at their feet, joy-fully snaking Spandex pants on over their workaday pantyhose.

No, no, and no, she thought, shaking her head at the rampant fashion victimization occurring all around her. *Y'know, if more people read* W *and had, well, personal shoppers, many of these terrible blunders could be avoided.*

She looked at a skirt, sighed, and put it back. No place to wear it at the moment. And that suede jacket thingie: too hot for L.A. weather by half.

Meanwhile: Angel. She'd done what he'd asked, but at a major inconvenience to herself and, poten-tially, to her career. In the old days she would have used her cell phone to make all the calls. And let Daddy pick up the bill. It was awkward to use the pay phone at the casting office, fumbling for change, knowing the others were trying to eaves-drop, learn about their competition, maybe catch a couple hints about another casting call. It kept pulling her out of the moment she was fighting so hard to stay in. Bright and cheery, loving mouth-wash more than life.

But her overall mood had not been the best. The Santa Ana—the hot winds that whistled down the canyons of Los Angeles and sucked the moisture out of every pore she owned—had given her a sinus headache. And, well, truth to tell, she had had the jitters. It happened when you constantly got rejected for every single thing you tried out for.

It almost made her feel sorry for the losers she used to routinely turn down when they'd ask her to dance at the Bronze.

On blistering, burning feet—*stupid cheap shoes!*—she left the Cooper Building behind. She started meandering around Fashion Alley, where the racks of clothes were crammed together right out on the street. It was a jostle, people milling and squeezing by. The B.O. level was instense.

Some touristy-looking women in oversize T-shirts and leggings—*so* over, even in the land of over, which had to be someplace like Michigan—posed for photos in front of a slightly more picturesque building than the others. Most of them—the buildings, not the women—were warehouses and factories built in the twenties, of brick, which you did not see much of in Southern California because of earthquakes.

One of the women in the group said, "Let's eat at the Pantry! Their mayor owns it."

Cordelia wondered if she'd ever be able to afford a vacation again in her life. She said again, with feeling, "My breath is so fresh!"

She slumped. "But basically, I stink."

There was not going to be a callback on this audition. Cordelia could tell by the way the casting director had glazed over while she was auditioning. Or maybe it had been the way she interrupted Cordelia and said, "Next."

What was it this time? Cordelia had almost demanded. *Is my nose too big? Is my nose too small? It's always something in this town.*

She stopped along the street and wiped her hair away from her forehead. Her calves were aching. The balls of her feet were on fire. *Stupid shoes.* It was going to be a stupid commercial, anyway. She would have been embarrassed to be in it.

In Sunnydale I was the standard by which all other Sunnydale High girls were judged. On the Cordelia Chase scale of one to ten, I was a twelve.

But in Hollywood—just two hours away from her hometown, but truly, on another planet, and she didn't mean the restaurant chain that Arnold, Bruce, and Demi owned—she was not being treated like the Rainbow Fish, the one everybody hated because it was so much more beautiful. She barely rated guppy attention. One casting director had told Cordelia's manager that her eyebrows were too bushy. Her *eyebrows*, which were totally waxable.

Noses were loppable. Teeth were cap-able. You could get your eyelids permanently tattooed. You could add collagen to your lips, suck the fat out of your chin, do a tuck, a lift, or a total sculpture. In Los Angeles you could do just about anything to the human body—if you had the bucks—to improve your looks. Or unimprove them, even, with all that gross piercing and stuff.

So she had to believe it wasn't any part of her body that was actually wrong, since she was basically gorgeous, and more than willing to do the plastic surgery thing. None of her rejections ever included anything about her acting ability, so it had to be something the casting directors couldn't put into words.

She could.

It's my clothes.

In the old days—that was to say, when she used to live in Sunnydale, and her parents had not lost all their money to the greedy IRS, who for sure had plenty of other people to shake down for whatever tiny deficit her non-taxpaying father had accumulated—she had shopped for many reasons. For fun. To maintain the high standards she had previously set. To raise the fashion bar at Sunnydale High (*so* not difficult).

She had also shopped because hey, let's face it, hanging out with Buffy and the rest of the "Scooby Gang"—quote marks added to not display amusement—had been very tough on her wardrobe. She didn't know how many beautiful things she had tossed because she couldn't get the bloodstains out.

So maybe Buffy and Willow had had something

going with their cheesy outfits. Demon slime and monster guts were much easier to remove from polyester blends than natural fibers. And if they weren't, no big trauma if you dressed for less.

But now, when the people around her really mattered, when they knew fashion as well as she did, she didn't have the money to look like a million bucks. She didn't have the money to look like fifty cents.

"Like I can afford anything better than last season's knockoff of the trend two years ago," she huffed as she pulled a strangely green silk blouse from an overcrowded circular rack marked with a cardboard sign AS IS—ALL SALES FINAL.

No wonder it's on sale. It's the ugliest color I've ever seen. It would make me look like a zombie.

And I know what I'm talking about.

Tears welled in her eyes. She was dying for nice new clothes and shoes and to have a latte whenever she wanted one. Shopping was just one more pleasure denied her, and it only served to remind her that she was on the fast track to nowhere.

"*Ibu*, please, no," said a man.

Cordelia jerked and looked up.

Whoa. She blinked in astonishment. *Hello, exciting new taste sensation.*

The young man who took the blouse from her was incredible to stare at. He looked to be in his mid-twenties, and he was extremely well put together despite his casual appearance. She knew a fifty-dollar cotton T-shirt when she saw one. His black jeans were bun-hugging tight, and his scuffed cowboy boots were perfect. He reeked of money, and a hint of Bijan for Men. Tall, his unlined skin was the color of cocoa butter, and his features were Brad-Pitt sharp and angled. Beneath short, spiked black hair, his deep brown eyes were almond-shaped. He looked like Harrison Ford, only if Harrison Ford was still in his mid-twenties and had been born in, say, Japan.

"That color's going to kill your complexion," he said. Smiling gently to take the sting out of his criticism, he shoved the blouse back into the tangle of coat hangers dripping with more ugly blouses and yet uglier sweaters.

"Uh," she said, too mesmerized to respond. Was someone shooting a movie? Was she on *The Cordelia Show?*

Had she died and gone to heaven?

He cocked his head. *"Vous me comprenez?"*

He's French, she thought, delighted. *Oh, why did I ever think French was a dead language? Why didn't I at least do my nails in a different class?*

"Um, I'm an American," she replied, in English.

Moving back into her native tongue, hunkily accented with, well, an accent, he said, "Sorry to be

54

so blunt. But my family's in the rag trade, and I know clothes." He shrugged. "But of course, it's up to you."

He inclined his head and started to walk away.

"Wait!" she cried. "I knew that color sucked." She cleared her throat and gestured at the rack. "There's too much yellow in it."

He brightened. "Too much yellow."

"I'd go all sallow." She nodded eagerly.

"It would be a disaster." He smiled and touched his palms together. "I'm Jusef Rais." He said it like she should know who that was; which, if he had been someone big in the *entertainment* industry, she would. She read Ted Casablancas's E! Online gossip report on Angel's computer every day.

"Hi." She started to copy his gesture, but about halfway through it, she decided that would be hokey. So she just kind of gave her hands a little wave and smiled.

"There's nothing on this entire rack that would suit you," he said. "These are clothes for bank tellers." He sniffed. "Clerical workers."

No need to mention I'm a receptionist, she thought. *Especially since it's just to help Angel out until I hit the big time.*

And, well, okay, so I can eat.

She ventured, "So you're here to . . . ?"

"I'm meeting someone."

"Oh." She was disappointed. *Figures*.

He smiled at her. "And I have."

She shoots, she scores, Cordelia thought happily. *At last!*

"Do you shop here often?" she asked, flirting.

He chuckled. "No. We own a lot of businesses in the area, though. I come in here now and then just to keep up."

A lot of businesses? A lot of them? Despite her euphoria, she wrinkled her nose. "Keep up with what? What people should *not* be buying?"

"You could say that. I stopped you from buying that blouse, didn't I?"

She was mildly defensive. "Like I said, I knew it sucked."

"You should come by our showroom sometime," he continued. "We specialize in Indonesian fabrics. Batik. It's coming back in."

"Yes." She nodded, although she didn't have the slightest idea what "batik" was. "It's really, um, beautiful. I love it."

"We're teaching our employees how to make it here."

As opposed to where? "Great," she enthused.

He cocked his head. "You're an actress, aren't you? I've seen you in something."

"Probably not. I do a lot of indie stuff. Independent," she amended. "Like you see in Landmark

56

Theaters." *If only.* "But not, um, you know, movies about lesbians or anything like that."

"We have a small studio back in Indonesia. In Dakarta."

"Oh." She raised her brows. *A studio? He owns a whole studio? Indonesia . . . where the heck's Indonesia? They must not have a Club Med or I'd know. Who could have guessed some of the useless factoids they taught in high school would actually be useful?*

Like French? Or geography?

"Any movies I would have seen?" she asked him.

"Not really." He grinned at her. "We produce a lot of indie stuff, as you say, only in foreign languages. Mandarin. Tagalog. And of course, Bahasa Indonesia."

"Oh, of course." She nodded as if she had a slight clue what he was talking about.

"I'm serious. I'm not trying to hit on you. I'm sure you meet guys all the time who tell you they're in the industry."

"Oh, of course." She made a careless gesture. "At all the parties. That I go to, with lots of other working professionals. You know how it is." Yeah, the parties she wasn't getting to attend anymore because she worked for Angel. Who could only work at night. When the parties were.

"Maybe you could work with us on something."

He reached in his pocket and handed her a business card. Their fingers brushed, and she nearly dropped it.

Talk about sizzle. As in, good thing it's a bone-dry day, or I'd get electrocuted.

From the look on his face, he'd felt it, too. Cordelia looked down at the card to mask her reaction. She used to be the Queen of Cool, until she got rusty from being ignored in Los Angeles. The lettering was gold and impossible to read. There was a rooster or something on it. She decided to examine it more closely later; she unzipped her purse and cheerily dropped it in.

"Well," Jusef said. He looked around. "It looks like my cousin isn't going to show." There was an edge to his voice that hadn't been there before. His eyes narrowed and disapproval rolled off him in waves.

"I've kept you from your shopping," he added.

"No, that's okay," she said. "Like you said, there's really nothing here and . . ." Her eyes widened. He was wearing a Rolex. *A beautiful, expensive Rolex.*

When she realized he was noticing her noticing, she said, "Oh, my, look at the time. It's almost sundown."

"Your Filofax is calling." He paused. His eyes glittered as his face shifted back into flirtatious mode. "Have you got a date?"

As if. Talking to him was the closest thing she'd had to a date in months.

It's just gotta be my clothes.

"Slamet, there you are," Jusef said as a guy rushed up to the two of them.

"Jusef, where the hell have you been?" new guy demanded.

"Waiting right here, just as we agreed."

"Don't be stupid. I was at the front door."

Cordelia stared. He could almost be a twin of Jusef—in other words, incredibly good-looking—except that he looked way beyond shut down. His eyes were swollen—from crying, she guessed—and his clothes, a really beautiful gunmetal gray business suit, looked like he had taken a spinning class in them.

New guy—Salami?—said gruffly, "I don't mean to be rude," he began, then stopped. He blinked at Cordelia. "My God, she looks exactly like Meg," he said.

Jusef shrugged. "A little. And it occurs to me I don't even know her name."

"Cordelia Chase," she told him and Salami.

"An actress," Jusef filled in.

"Oh." Salami cared less than not.

There was a pause. Then Jusef said, "My father died earlier today."

And you're not sorry, she thought. Still, because it was the right thing to do, she touched her chest and said, "I'm so sorry. Truly."

He put on a sad face, too. "My dad was getting on. But it's always shocking when death snatches a soul from the world. You know what I mean?"

"Um, yes." *Unless it's a monster's soul. Although most of them don't have souls. Which is part of what being a monster's all about. Besides killing people.*

He regarded her intently. "Somebody like you, what would you know about death and dying?"

Got a few hours? she thought, but she said, "I might surprise you."

"We must go," Salami announced.

Cordelia turned to Jusef. "It's been . . . nice . . . chatting about ugly clothes."

Jusef cupped her elbow and led her a few steps out of earshot. "My father's burial may be attended by close family members only," he said. "But may I invite you to the *sedhekah?*"

She hesitated. "I guess it depends on what it is."

"It's a traditional prayer meal for the dead, to pay our respects." He held out a hand. "Since we're fairly Westernized, there will also be a much larger reception for my family's business associates. They'll both be held on our compound."

"Your compound," she said slowly.

"In Indonesia, we invite everyone to funeral receptions. The larger the gathering, the more honor the family receives. You'd be most welcome," he told her.

"At your father's funeral."

"Yes." He was entirely serious.

"Well."

His smile was amazing. He gave his nose a slight wrinkle. "For me? It would do me honor."

C'mon, do it, she told herself. *Free food and cute guys. Cute guys who make movies and have business associates and a compound.*

It's only slightly weird.

Right?

"I'll have to check in with my boss, I mean my service," she said. Successful L.A. actresses did not moonlight as receptionists.

"You're a cautious girl. I like that." He pointed to her purse. "My numbers are on my card. Including my cell phone." He patted his shirt pocket, and she saw the thin bulge of something state-of-the-art. "We have at least three hours before the *sedhekah*. Slamet and I are just now going back to the house to wash the body in preparation for the burial."

Eww. Too much information.

It occurred to her that she had never actually washed a dead body. She had recently put pieces of one back together like a jigsaw puzzle, and back in Sunnydale, she was always finding them in the most inconvenient places—the caf fridge, Aura's gym locker, the backseat of her car. But washing one was new to her.

"It's a ritual," he told her. "My family is very big on ritual." He smiled like someone having a private joke.

"Okay," she managed weakly.

"Call in three hours, then," he suggested. "It will be quite all right. I'll send a car if you are able to attend."

As in a limo? Are happy days here again?

"I'm a stranger," she pointed out. "I mean, this is kind of a family affair"—*a rich family affair, so shut up!*—"and what should I wear?"

"Something black, if you have it." He gave her a once-over that made her cheeks burn. "You must look wonderful in black."

"I do," she agreed.

He laid a hand on her forearm. His nails were impeccable.

A few paces away, just out of hearing range, Salami paced. He looked royally pissed off. *Maybe he's jealous,* she thought hopefully. *Or maybe if I show at the Neil Sedaka–thing, the family will, like, curse me or something.*

"I could use someone in my cheering section," he added. "I'm kind of the family black sheep."

"Oh. Well. I'm a cheerful girl, they always say." She held out her hand. "I'll do my best."

"Thanks." He gave her a sad-boy smile. "I don't know if you believe in karma, but I do."

"I'm not sure." She moved her shoulders. "Sometimes it seems like some people have more than their share of bad luck." *Like me with my acting career.*

"And also, good luck," she quickly added, because of course, that was where he was going.

"Let's find out if our meeting was good luck. I don't believe it was an accident that you pulled out that hideous blouse when I first looked over at you." He took her hand.

Salami waved at him. "Jusef, we must go."

"All right, Slamet," he said.

"Oh, it's *Slamet*," she murmured.

"It means 'good fortune' in Indonesian."

"Mine means Cordelia."

Jusef looked hard at her. She felt as if she was swimming in his rich dark brown eyes. *Accent on rich.* "You'd better call."

"Okay," she croaked.

"Give us three hours," he reminded her. "I'll turn the phone off while we bury him."

She nodded, a little grossed out.

Actually, a lot.

"Good luck," she said. Then, as casually as she could, she turned slowly on her high, high heels and walked away.

I'm going on a date to a funeral. Only in L.A., she thought. *Of course, also in Sunnydale, but then, these guys would be, like, demons in disguise or something.*

She glanced over her shoulder, mildly disappointed to see them heading in the opposite direction. It was time for her to get going anyway. Angel would be awake soon, and she wanted to find out if his Nira had called him. And who she was.

She was about halfway to the bus stop—as humiliating as it was in Los Angeles to be car-free, she was—when she felt a tug at her purse.

"Hey," she said, jerking it toward her. She glanced down to see a very tiny child with a very tiny hand firmly inside her purse. She realized she had left it unzipped when she'd dropped Jusef's card into it.

Solemnly the little girl stared up at Cordelia. Her face was moon-shaped and her eyes were two dark crescents. Her long black hair was caught up in two ponytails. Her front teeth were missing. She had on raspberry tie-dyed shorts and a sleeveless top, which made her look very cute and not at all like a little thief.

Slowly she withdrew her hand.

"Were you trying to steal something out of my purse?" Cordelia demanded.

The girl kept staring at her. Cordelia frowned. "You speakie English?"

Still staring.

Cordelia felt unnerved. She said, "Don't do it

again. It's wrong. You'll get in bad trouble. The police will throw you in jail. Bad girl."

Cordelia made a show of zipping up her purse. "No, no." She wagged her finger and kept walking.

After about five seconds she looked back.

The little girl was still staring after her.

Then she was joined by a boy who was slightly taller than she. He also wore tie-dyed clothes, in his case dark blue and white. He smacked the little girl hard against the cheek. The girl staggered backward but remained silent.

Cordelia shouted, "Hey!"

The little girl turned her attention back to Cordelia. Blood trickled from the corner of her mouth down her chin. The boy started pulling on her arm. Then he began yelling at her in a foreign language. When she didn't respond, he hit her again.

But her gaze was still focused on Cordelia as blood dripped from her chin to her colorful top.

"Stop it, you little bully!" Cordelia cried. She ran toward the two little children.

An oncoming pedestrian—a stooped woman with close-cropped gray hair—blocked her path.

"Excuse me," Cordelia said, agitated, and swerved around her.

The two children had disappeared, practically into thin air.

Perplexed, Cordelia looked from side to side,

then made a little circle. There was no way they could have just run off. She would have seen them.

The gray-haired woman thrust a hand at her and said, "Money?" She had almond-shaped eyes and a round face. She looked tired and haggard.

"All I have is bus fare," Cordelia said.

"You, rich girl," the woman accused. She held out her hand. "Money."

"Hey, back off." Cordelia took a step away. "I don't have any money, okay? Just bus fare."

Just then, the two little kids appeared out of nowhere, barreling toward Cordelia. As she glanced at them, the old woman grabbed her purse. She put it under her arm like a linebacker and took off at a dead heat into an alley. The two children followed after, darting along like baby gazelles.

"Hey!" Cordelia shouted.

She clattered after them in her ridiculous high heels, realized she was going to either lose her purse or break her ankles, and stopped long enough to kick off her shoes. The three figures were getting tinier and tinier as she swept down gracefully the way she'd learned in modeling school back when her parents could afford such things, grabbed her shoes, and started after them.

"That's my bus fare!" she bellowed.

A really dirty man with a vacant stare silently watched her pass. She frowned at him.

"Help me!"

"Got change? I'm a veteran," he said.

She flew past him. Filth crusted her stockinged feet. She gagged but kept going.

A field of broken glass sparkled before her. She put on the brakes and squinted into the alley. There was nothing to see but darkness. Nothing to hear but the dirty man shambling up behind her.

"You got change?" he asked her.

She regarded him. "No," she said. "But I bet *you* do." She held out her hand. "Give me thirty-five cents."

The man blinked at her.

That was when the screaming started.

CHAPTER FOUR

"As we used to say in the auld country," Doyle said to Angel, "yuck."

The two stood in Angel's office. Near dusk, Angel had stirred from a mishmash of dreams that included hell, fire, and the dancing woman dressed in gold.

Also, the Chihuahua from the Taco Bell commercials.

Now he and Doyle were looking at the autopsy photos that Angel had managed to download from the police department's pathology lab. Kate didn't know he could—and did—do this on a fairly routine basis whenever she mentioned anything out of the ordinary at a crime scene.

"*Yuck*'s a word," Angel replied. He looked from the photo to the clock on the wall. "Where's Cordelia? She's late."

"Maybe she got the part," Doyle said hopefully.

Doyle had this thing for Cordelia. Angel had no idea if it would ever go anywhere. His fellow Irishman wasn't rich, and so far he had kept the fact that he was half-demon under wraps. Perhaps on account of the fact that Cordy had never had one single good word to say about demons.

"That would be good," Angel said.

Doyle frowned. "But she'd call us to tell us, wouldn't she? I mean, we're her closest friends. Maybe she didn't get the part. Maybe she's in a terrible dive of a pub, drowning her sorrows." He looked worried.

"Cordelia Chase?" Angel shook his head. "She wouldn't be caught dead alone in a bar. Even if she was old enough to drink." He shifted. "Let's give her a few more minutes."

"Before what?" Doyle asked unhappily. He picked up the phone. "I'll call her place."

"Good idea," Angel said.

He shifted his attention back to the computer screen. The image in the color shot, while gut-wrenching, was also mildly familiar. He couldn't bring to mind the time and place, but he'd seen something like this before.

Trust Kate not to trust me enough to tell me everything, he thought, smiling grimly. Okay, burn victim; she hadn't lied, but it was so much more than that.

Angel knew—but wasn't precisely certain how he knew—that this person had been burned from the inside out.

So, can a burning body ignite an apartment building?

"I'm getting her machine," Doyle reported. He said into the mouthpiece, "Cordelia, it's Doyle. We're a bit worried about you. If you're not coming in soon, let us know, okay? Did I mention that it's Doyle?"

Angel smiled to himself. *As if it could be anyone else with that accent.*

"Was that a person at one time?" Doyle queried as he hung up.

"It was," Angel said. With the mouse, he moved the cursor over the black and red portions in the lower left corner of the screen.

He added, "Kate told me she's had some strange homicides. I'm wondering if this is the body she found in Nira's building last night."

"What do you think?" Doyle asked, grimacing.

Angel stared hard at the photograph as slowly, images began to take form in his mind. They weren't from his dreams, and there were no Chihuahuas in them.

"Spontaneous human combustion?" Doyle suggested in the ensuing silence. "You ever read about that? It happens."

"Yes. It happens," Angel replied slowly.

The images were Angel's memories, long suppressed. Allowing them entrance, he began to remember a lot more than he'd ever thought he'd want to.

Than he ever would allow himself.

"Angel?" Doyle asked. "You think that's what this is about?"

His Irish lilt took Angel back to Galway and when he was still human.

The memories clicked.

Galway, 1752

"Granny Quinn's dead. Let's go and make a wish on her corpse," Doreen Kenney whispered to Angelus as she pushed him coyly away.

They were lying in the hay in her father's barn. The sun had almost set, and the crimson beams gleamed through the upper doors of the loft. Doreen's hair was a fiery red, proof, some said, that she was a sorceress. Angelus half-believed it. Her merest glance set him aflame.

"Granny's dead, and there's nothing more to be done with her bones but pray over them," Angelus said, impatient with her. "Sure and we've both done enough praying for the dead in our lifetimes. For them we loved. For family and friends. What's that old hag to us?"

Death was a constant companion in Galway; babes and children and the old folks dying, beggars starving, and sickness coming oftener than not. No house was spared forever, be it Catholic or Protestant. No man, be he aristocrat or tenant farmer.

"Moira said sure and if you wish on the dead when they're laid out, you'll have what you want."

"And if that were so, would Moira be an old maid of nineteen?" Angelus scoffed.

Doreen looked puzzled. Angelus had always thought she was a bit thick; not a bad thing in a female, to be sure, as you did not want them thinking too much on things. Women had better things to do—looking after their men and taking care of their babies.

But Dorrie was rather like a colt, in that you were never certain if her mind would go to the place you were trying to lead her, or amble on the way, forgetting what she was about.

"What I'm saying is, Moira's had lots of chances to make quite a few wishes," Angel explained. "And we both know she's not got a single suitor. Nor like to have one, with those teeth of hers." He shivered. "And that breath."

"That's cruel," she said. Then she grinned. "But it's truth. But Granny Quinn could remedy that. I'm sure of it."

"It's a freezing day," Angelus continued, "and we've better things to do than mock the corpse of the village wise woman."

"Wise woman? She were a witch, and you know it," Doreen said, pouting. "Her damned spirit will rise tonight and meet the Devil in the wood. She'll fly off with him, naked on a broomstick." Her green eyes gleamed with excitement.

"Ah, Doreen, me own enchantress, and if you'd only fly naked on *my* broomstick," he quipped, catching up her hand, trying to place it where he would benefit most.

She burst into giggles and yanked her hand away. "Angelus, you know I've got my virtue still, and I'll not give it to a man who isn't my husband."

"Sure and you delight in my suffering," he moaned. "My father won't give me the means to have a wife. If he has his way, I've years left as his dependent."

"I haven't years left," she said pointedly. Her father was a very rich man, and she had a sizable dowry. Old Patrick Kenney wanted her married off while she was still in her prime; she was sixteen, and it was high time for her to find a suitable husband. As landed gentry himself, Angelus could be that husband, if his reputation didn't precede him. Patrick Kenney thought him nothing but a wastrel and a scoundrel.

The gentleman's opinion being truth, on both counts.

"Doreen, if I could, I would." He slipped his hand around her waist. "This very moment."

Giggling, she pressed against him. "Yes, you would, Angelus. Of that, I've no doubt." He caught his breath.

"But you may *not*. However," she continued, before he had a chance to protest, "take me to Granny Quinn's, and you can make a wish that may come true."

She kissed him full and deep; if she had asked him to dig up the entire churchyard in that moment to procure for her a hand of glory, he would have agreed.

" 'Tis said you're a witch yourself," he whispered.

She tensed. "Take that back, Angelus." Her voice was as cold as stone. "Take it back, or never speak another word to me as long as you live."

He blinked. "Sure, and you don't believe such things yourself."

"Not another word." She moved away from him, arranging her clothes as she stood.

At that very moment the sun disappeared, and the colors in the barn bled to gray.

Then it must have been a trick of the light, for over her face, he swore he saw another face, deformed, hideous, its glowing red eyes filled with rage. Transfixed, he stared, but when he blinked, there was naught there but his own lovely Doreen.

"Don't let us go," he blurted. "It would be bad luck."

She laughed at him full on. "What, and is himself a coward?" she taunted. "Then I'll find another who'll take me."

"No, you won't." He stood up.

Her gaze traveled over his body, and a smile played at her lips.

" 'Tis jealous you are, then?" she asked.

"Of course."

"Oh, Angelus, you're such a modest sort," she said gently, "if you're thinking jealousy is the order of the day."

He melted. He told himself firmly that the strange apparition was merely a trick of the light, and his own foolish imagination. The nights were long and he was bored with the world. Such a situation called for making things up to keep himself entertained—such as leaving Galway forever and making his fortune. Then he could have a woman like Doreen to wife.

"Doreen," he said feelingly, "I love you."

"Meself, and all the other colleens in Galway," she chided.

"No, and never," he said feelingly. "And I take back all I've ever said that may offend. Forgive me, dearest girl. You've got my heart."

"And your soul?"

He felt a wee chill. Nevertheless, he laughed. "If any but God may have it," he tossed off, "then it's yours for the having."

She turned her back to him and lifted her head. Through the window, the full moon glowed. He was surprised it had risen so quickly. Doreen's red hair now looked yellow in the light. He'd never told her so, but his preference was for fair-haired maids, not red hair nor black.

Still with her back to him, she said, "Come along, then. We'll see Granny Quinn and learn what you're about."

They took two of her father's fine horses, him on Chieftain and her on Black Silky, and as they galloped through the darkness, the salt and stink of the harbor thickened like a smoke. A strong wind furled Doreen's plaid cloak as Black Silky took on a pounding rhythm, hoofbeats heavy on the ebony earth. Her family was not so old as Angelus's own, but the Kenneys had always prospered. Some claimed the family—redheads all—trafficked with the spirits to gain their wealth, but educated folk ignored the cant of jealous gossips.

Clouds rushed overhead, as if chasing the two of them, and Angelus put his spurs to his horse.

"Doreen," he shouted, "a storm's coming in!"

She galloped farther ahead of him. He couldn't tell if she chose to ignore him or couldn't hear him. Her cloak billowed out like the wings of a great bird; she hunkered down as the horse gained speed, and as she raced along, she looked as if she were headless.

Lightning crackled overhead. Chieftain threw back his head and whinnied in fear. With a second crackle the clouds broke and rain began to fall. Steamy mist rose from the green hills, spreading across Angelus's path.

He had a thought to abandon the road for shelter. He was ashamed of his childish nerves, but every feeling within him was against this adventure. It were folly, sure, and nothing more, to press on in such weather.

Besides the which, he had an assignation to keep at Mistress Burton's Society House. Bess, his favorite, had no illusions about rings and vows, and she was nothing for tempting and taunting without the giving. . . .

Added to that, he wasn't sure he wanted to look at Granny Quinn's dead body. The old crone had lived quite alone, but that had never stopped her from talking to folk no others could see. There were stories of a lover who had proved unfaithful, and that his bones were buried in her garden. That on a winter midnight you could hear the wind whistle through his rib cage, and his teeth chatter from the cold.

Wives' tales, he told himself.

At that moment Doreen wheeled her horse around and waved at him to make haste. He couldn't see her face in the darkness and the wind, but somehow, of a certainty, he knew she was laughing at him.

Irritated, he spurred his horse on.

Her hovel was a poor one, was Granny Quinn's. Things skittered in the trash heap beside it. The place stank of peat, mud, and the carcasses of small animals draped over a line like Sunday wash just outside the door.

The house's sad weathered stones piled one atop the other flickered yellow from a large bonfire in the garden. Angelus remembered the old ways, when bonfires were lit to warm the dead as they groped their way to the deadlands.

There was a group around it of at least six or seven people. All but one were women, and four or five of the females pressed handkerchiefs against their faces. They were weeping. Another had covered her mouth with the tip of her shawl, and she was keening loud enough to wake the dead.

Angelus was surprised; he had not thought there'd be much in the way of mourners, paid professionals or otherwise. Those who came to visit Granny Quinn did so on dark, moonless nights. From shame, they kept themselves well hidden. They crept to her door and whispered their requests—for love potions, remedies, and poisons.

Her face flickering between the flames of the fire, the woman who had covered her mouth with her shawl began singing in the ancient tongue. Angelus listened, and further puzzled: She was a *bean caointe*, a professional mourner. He was certain of that, and yet her death song was for a drowned child.

The sole man was dressed like an Aran fisherman. He wore a black-brimmed hat and his light-colored clothes were stiff and rough. As he turned to face Angelus, the mystery of the keeners and the death song was solved: He held in his arms a dead child in a white petticoat—a boy of four or five, by its look.

Kelp was still wrapped around the child's neck, and his tiny feet were blue from the cold. Silently the fisherman stared at Angelus, and then a single tear ran down his cheek.

Dismounting in a hop, Doreen took no note of the tragic scene. Eagerly she bobbed around the bonfire and scurried into Granny Quinn's hovel.

But despite himself, Angelus was transfixed. Still astride Chieftain, he stared back at the fisherman, who never spoke a word. His dead child in his arms, he stood like a stone statue on a grave.

This man is dead, just like his child, Angelus thought. *And I'm dying, here in Galway. Day by day. There's nothing for me here besides wenching and quarreling with my father, himself a dead man.*

The keening of the wailing women rose, punctuated by the crackling of the bonfire. They sang on, and Angelus listened despite himself, entranced. Finally he stirred, feeling as if he had lost himself for a time; he stirred and looked through the flames to the canted door of the hovel, wondering what Doreen was doing in there. Praying, most like.

A sudden, bitter wind rushed over the scene, dragging a heavy net of darkness over the figures, faces cauled with shadow. The air became frigid and wintry in an instant.

The mourning women's voices broke off. As one, they crossed themselves and looked around in astonishment. There was no sound but the wailing of the wind and the beating of Angelus's own heart.

Until, low and eerie, came a baleful moan that sent a shudder down his spine. It began like a gathering fog upon the cold earth, then spiraled up, gaining height, becoming a shrill shriek that drowned out the frightened cries of the mourners.

The Aran fisherman shouted, "No! You can't have me Paddy!" He folded himself over the child and dropped to the ground in a tight, sheltering ball.

Angelus fought the rising gale to get to his side.

He put a hand on the man's shoulder and said, "What is it? What is that sound?"

"Are you not an Irishman, then?" the fisherman cried. " 'Tis the banshee, come to collect my boy! I come to wish on Granny's bones to give him back to me, but now the banshee will take him!" He began to sob. "Patrick! Oh, Paddy, don't go with her!"

The others started screaming.

Angelus rolled his eyes at the pure superstition of it. "It's the wind, man!" he bellowed.

The moan became a shriek. The wind was wild now, and the women scattered. Whipped into a frenzy, the bonfire gave off a shower of sparks like a comet. The fisherman raised his hand above his head, praying in Latin that was pitiable for its mangling.

Then Doreen staggered from the hovel. She stood with her profile to Angelus for a moment, and it looked jagged, somehow. Her hood shaded the space from her forehead to the bridge of her nose, but her cheeks and jawline were all wrong.

Very slowly she lifted her hands to the hood and dropped it backward. At the same time she made a quarter-turn and faced the bonfire. She gazed full on at the fire. Her face was ashen, and there were black circles under her eyes. Her lips were gray.

Her fiery hair had turned pure white.

Angelus gaped at her. "Dorrie?" he murmured, though no one, least of all she, could hear him.

Unsteadily, he planted one foot beneath himself, hoisting up to a standing position like an old man with severe gout. The wind was so cold his young joints were aching. The spittle on his lips froze to ice.

Her gaze moved from the fire to him. She raised a hand and extended a finger. Slowly she began to walk, staggering forward in a shuffle that was hideous to watch.

"The banshee!" the fisherman screamed, clutching at his child. "No, no! God and all His angels have my Paddy in their care!" He looked frantically at Angelus. "He's not baptized! She'll take him!"

Angelus stared open-mouthed at Doreen. He had never been more frightened in his life.

Doreen—or whatever she had become—shouted a word in a language he didn't understand, and the wind stopped. The fisherman was babbling and crying, clutching his babe. She stared at them, and then her face broke into a hideous smile.

All but a handful of her teeth were gone.

"Angelus," she said. "Wish. Wish that I am young, and beautiful, and your bride." She held out her arms. "Wish, and it shall be yours."

He couldn't move, couldn't speak. She took another step toward him. Angelus found his legs and darted backward. He made the sign against the evil eye.

She walked closer.

The fisherman raised anguished eyes to him. "Wish that she spares my child," he begged.

The figure looked first as the fisherman, and then at his dead son. As if it were all the same to her, she shrugged.

"That can be your wish," she told Angelus. "One wish, while I stand." She moved her hips. "Or you may have Doreen, and all her wealth. Only say it."

"For my child, man!" the father pleaded. "Save the soul of my child!"

Angelus stirred. *It's a dream,* he told himself, *a nightmare, sure and it is.* But he knew he was awake.

A trick, then. Didn't I see this same face over hers, back in the barn? Her sisters and she are having a laugh at my expense. I don't know how, but there is no such thing as magic. I've never believed in it, and I don't believe in it now—

"You needn't believe," the specter said, as if she had read his mind. " 'Tis not required. Only the doing. You have the means to change your life forever. You need only speak, Angelus."

He squared his shoulders and licked his lips. "Speakin' requires believing."

"For the love of God, man!" the anguished fisherman cried. "Tell her to go away!"

"Is it Doreen and her dowry you want?" Her voice was a whisper, yet he could hear each word distinctly, as if her gray lips were pressed against his ear. "Or to leave Galway forever? You fancy London, I believe. You can have London. And Paris. And even the Colonies."

"I'll make my own way," Angelus said defiantly.

She laughed, and it was a horrible sound, like the death rattle of a woman in terrible pain. "You cannot make your way out of the schoolyard, Master Angelus. You're a liar, and a cheat, and you've stolen all that you can from your own father, without him turning you out for a common thief. Your mother's heart is broken, though your sister loves you still.

"And you've broken the hearts of many maids, some of whom have found their way to this very door, to rid themselves of your get. So in your own way, you're a murderer, to boot."

She lifted a bony finger. "And you'll die for murder, one day. You'll suffer for all you've done, in ways you cannot fathom and I cannot even tell."

She jabbed her finger in his direction. "And you'll die alone, and none will grieve ye."

At her words the fisherman made the sign to ward off the evil eye in Angelus's direction. Angelus ran a hand through his hair and gave his head a nervous shake. It was often said that dead eyes could see the future. So he was to hang for murder, was he?

Anger flashed through him. *This is all a sham,* he

told himself. *Doreen's family is rich; they can hire fine charlatans to frighten away suitors they don't approve of.*

"Then I'll not die," he flung at her. "I'll never die. That's my wish."

She cackled. "Foolish creature! You've sealed your doom, then. For know this, me fine-spirited lad: God's children die. All of them. Them that doesn't die are not His. They belong to the Devil."

As she spoke, she glanced at the dead child. The boy's father clung to him and shouted, "Archangel Michael! Saint Patrick! Help me in my need!"

The woman laughed again. "Young da," she said, and for him her voice was gentle, "your wee one's soul's already in Heaven. God covets the innocent, and that child surely was. Whist your blatherin' and hie ye home."

"Merciful God," the man murmured, crossing himself. He staggered to his feet, turned, and ran.

She looked back at Angelus. "That leaves just you for the banshees and the Great Hunt. Soon enough, you'll be fodder for demons."

"Not I, you hag!" he shouted.

In an eyeblink the wind picked up again. It was fiercer than anything Angelus had ever encountered, even at sea. It pulled at him and he fought against it.

It lifted Doreen—or whoever she was—straight

into the air and landed her square in the center of the bonfire.

In a trice she went up in flames. She screamed and struggled; hair, clothes, face—all were consumed in an instant.

The fire raged; it became a mountain of flame, roaring straight up to the heavens; through fog and moonlight, until it extended beyond Angelus's range of vision. He imagined they could see it all the way to Dublin. It was like the tail of a comet.

It was like a bridge to Hell.

Angelus tried to mount his horse, but the beast would have none of that. It whinnied and reared, turned tail, and cantered away. Black Silky ran after, and the horses disappeared into the darkness.

"Damn you!" Angelus shouted at them.

The fire went out. All at once there was nothing, not even a burning ember. It was as if there had never been a fire.

Except for the body that smoldered in the moonlight. Except for that.

Tentatively he approached it. The light was dim, but what he saw, he never told another soul: The body had somehow melted into itself, although the facial features remained intact. It was as if a candle had burned from the inside out, leaving the decorative exterior for last.

Speechless, he turned and fled into the night.

✦   ✦   ✦

It took him all night and half the next day to get back to Galway, and when asked where he had been, he made up a lie about falling asleep drunk in a ditch. Better drunk than crazy.

Doreen Kenney was never seen again, and though a search was made, no one looked in at Granny Quinn's. And to Angelus's knowledge, no one ever went to Granny Quinn's again, ever, not even to bury what was there.

A fortnight later he became Angelus, the One with the Angelic Face, the most ruthless vampire who had ever lived.

If what he was could be considered alive.

CHAPTER FIVE

> "Are you man or beast?"
> "Man."
> "What's your name?"
> "I've lost it."
> —ancient Indonesian *barong*, or dance

Nias, 1863

"Latura," the Servant whispered as the head-hunters converged on her. She closed her eyes and flinched as a spear sliced so close to her throat that she felt the pressure in the air.

He had sent demons. He had sent flames. Surely he would not fail her now.

"Latura, aid your Servant," she murmured.

The headhunters drew back. Their fierce faces were pinched and wary. Mumbling to each other, they sank one by one to their knees and put their foreheads to the earth.

A weight settled on her shoulder; she slid her gaze toward it and stifled the scream in her throat. What was there was hideous. Neither hand nor talon, nor claw or any other thing she could describe, yet it served the purpose of a hand. It was leathery and dark green, and yet, as she stared—unable to tear her gaze away—it shifted and transformed. It looked almost like a face, and then it became long, ropelike tentacles that flailed and flapped. It was purple, noxious mist, and then it was trickling liquid that reeked of the dead.

She was somewhere alone as it seeped inside her. She floated in darkness, unable to breathe; she felt it moving through her body. Icy cold congealed her blood; for two, three, four beats, her heart stopped, unable to give her life.

The god has forsworn me, she thought desperately as she began to die.

Then she rose from the ground and soared through the air. Her heart began to beat again; for a moment she thought she herself was flying. Then she realized that something had hold of her clothing, and it was carrying her through the air.

She looked behind and up.

It was an enormous winged serpent. Its face was huge, its eyes glowing red, its snout fanged. Teeth as long as her forearms had sliced through her blouse, and she hung by tattered ribbons of fabric high above the ground, higher still.

She cried out as she and the monster soared above the throng of warriors, higher still, until it seemed she would be able to touch the face of the moon with her fingertips.

When she looked back over her shoulder, there were flickering yellow dots on the ground. She looked harder. They were the warriors, each one on fire. In their agony they were running to quench the flames.

"No," she whispered, but deep inside her soul she heard the god answer, *Yes*.

Los Angeles, the present

It was the custom in Indonesia for observant families to care for their dead themselves. For them to wash and perfume the body with their own hands. To wrap their deceased in linens. If they cremated their dead, for them to light the match.

If they buried their dead, for them to shovel the earth and put the body in.

In a dark room choked with incense, the two male Rais cousins attended to the bathing of Bang Rais's corpse.

Meg wasn't sure if they knew she was there. As Jusef's protégée—and lover—she was allowed to come and go as she pleased. She often came into this room to meditate, as Jusef had taught her; to keep the memories at bay and stay in the moment.

It had been very dim and quiet; she had sat by the fountain with its floating lotuses, and then, almost overcome by tiredness, she had stretched out on some satin pillows behind it, dozing. Tonight would be the *sedhekah,* and the reception, and she would dance in the old way, the *barong,* before . . .

Before . . .

No, she thought, and let everything go.

She let sleep come.

When she awakened, the Rais patriarch was laid out naked on lengths of yellow and red silk near the entrance to the room. She sat up, unseen because of the wall around the fountain, unnoticed because death was in the room, and death was always jealous of attention.

Bang Rais. He's really dead, she thought, shivering. There were many in her country who believed he would never die. She'd already heard on the news that at least a dozen people had committed suicide out of despair that he was gone.

He looked as powerful in death as he had in life. Unusually tall for an Indonesian—six foot three—muscular from working out, jaw firm and face chiseled from plastic surgery, he had been a vigorous man.

It had been a shock when his heart had stopped beating. There had been no warning, no lingering illness. According to Jusef, who had been with him when he died—in his room, chatting with his son about the future of Indonesia—there hadn't even been a moment where his left arm had tingled or he had complained of chest pains. He had been, and then he had ceased to be.

Many thousands of Indonesians had prayed to their gods that he would take over their country. President, dictator, king, god—they didn't care how he styled himself. If only he would lead them, and feed them, and keep their children from dying of preventable diseases.

What would happen to Indonesia now?

What will happen to the band? Will Jusef have to take over the family, or will Slamet still run things?

Meg watched as the two cousins washed the corpse. Jusef dipped the ladle into a large glass bowl of water. Fresh yellow plumeria blossoms with red centers floated in the water, giving the room a floral odor to mask the onset of decomposition.

Jusef poured the water over his father's chest. Slamet trailed his palm through the fragrant liquid, in a motion like wiping the condensation off a car window.

Then Jusef bent down to his father's ear and whispered, "What is it like, Father? Are you welcome in the deadlands, or are you a stranger there?"

"Don't," Slamet muttered. "We'll bring him back."

"We don't have the Book," Jusef said. "We don't know how. Besides, he's dead. We can't raise the dead. We can only make a living man immortal." He ladled more water. "And that's only in theory. After all, we haven't ever done it."

"You're glad," Slamet flung at him. "You can't even hide it."

"Of course I'm not." Jusef sighed. "After all this time. My father dropped dead."

"You know he couldn't die. You know the god favored him. Something's wrong. Someone is interfering with our magick."

"Slamet, it was the turn of the great wheel," Jusef said. "It was not his karma."

Slamet's right, Meg thought. *Jusef's glad his father's dead. But what are they talking about? What about bringing him back?*

Raising the dead? Immortality?

What book?

She began to tremble. A voice in her mind replied, *You know what book, Meg. Mary Margaret Taruma, you know.*

The trembling increased. She was falling into blackness, falling into memories. . . .

When she opened her eyes, Jusef was sitting in front of her with a candle in his hand. The warm yellow light cast blue-black highlights in his short hair.

"You okay, baby?" he asked her.

She blinked. "What happened?"

"You had a seizure," he told her. "Don't you remember?"

She shook her head. "I don't remember anything."

She looked around the room. They were in Jusef's quarters on the compound. The bed was rumpled. A pair of speakers and an amp were grouped in the vast, carpeted space between the bed and the large, spacious bathroom.

"We came in to work on the funeral dance," he reminded her. "You started having one of your seizures. I barely got it under control."

She touched her head. It was throbbing. "Thanks," she said softly.

"I have to help with the funeral preparations. I've called our doctor. You stay here and rest, all right?"

Something flickered in the back of her mind. Something about preparing for the funeral. Seated by the pond as he and Slamet talked about . . . about . . .

She strained to concentrate. Nothing came to her.

Jusef picked up her hand and kissed the back of it. "Rest, Meg."

She nodded and allowed him to settle her back on the bed. He fluffed up a pillow and slid it beneath her head. Then he tenderly drew the covers up beneath her chin and kissed her forehead.

"I'll be back later," he assured her. "Sleep, okay?"

"It must be getting worse," she said. "I haven't had a seizure in a long time."

"No," he insisted.

A sad smiled passed between them. About a year ago, shortly after they had met, Meg had begun having seizures. Specialists in Dakarta had discovered that Meg had a particular type of tumor in her brain. It was extremely rare for someone her age to have one. Among other things, it caused a buildup of fluid, which was drained via a small plastic tube that ran under her skin from her skull to her neck. If one knew where to look, one could see the slight rise of the tubing along the left side of her neck.

The tumor was inoperable. She had seen in her CAT scans that it was growing. Sooner or later, it would kill her.

Most of the time she was able to live a normal life. There were days when she forgot about it altogether. A lot of that was due to the hypnosis sessions Jusef conducted. At first he had used them to help her forget other things.

She closed her eyes.

And dreamed.

He was a man, yet not a man. He lived, and yet his heart did not beat.

If she called to him, he would come for her.

She opened her mouth and whispered, "Angel."

"What?" Angel asked as he came out of his reverie.

"I said, she's still not answering," Doyle answered.

Angel shook his head. The sounds of the city penetrated the last remnants of his memories of that strange night in Galway. He remembered every detail, down to clothes, smells, sensations; remembered, too, how he had tormented himself for years after he had first regained his soul. Endlessly scrutinizing each moment, turning the memories inside and out.

Had that wish, that night, brought his sire, Darla, into his life? Had that been the moment he had been damned?

There was no way to know, of course. *And it doesn't really matter, does it?*

Things are the way they are. I became, and am, whatever it is I am.

But the thing was, Angel couldn't stop thinking about it. Couldn't stop remembering. It was what the Gypsies wanted, wasn't it? For him to endlessly, obsessively, regret everything that led up to his transformation into one of the foulest creatures Hell ever spit back into the world?

Confession was supposed to be good for the soul. But what good could ever come of this torment?

It will keep me from ever doing it again, he

thought. As long as true happiness was denied him
—*or, as Doyle would say, as long as I deny myself
true happiness*—he would keep his soul. Remorse
was the quality that separated humans from the
demons, at least according to the Kalderash Gypsy
clan who had cursed him for murdering their
favorite daughter. Did it follow, then, that the
purest form of existence was suffering?

He could not, did not, believe that.

He said to Doyle, "It's not like her to not phone."

"And I've been saying that for the last five minutes," Doyle said impatiently. "You haven't been listening to a word I've said, have you?"

The phone rang. He and Doyle exchanged
relieved looks as Angel picked it up.

"Cordelia," Angel began.

"No, sorry. Kate," the police detective said. "I
think I've got a client of yours here. Which I find
extremely interesting."

"Nira? In custody?"

"In the morgue. New arrival. Well, we got the
body last night, but it's been a while on the ID."

On the other end she was shuffling papers. He
was positive she was talking about the victim whose
autopsy photo was up on his screen. It made him
wonder if she actually did know that he hacked
whenever he needed to. If this was her way of letting him know that she was aware of his activities.

"Thai," she filled in. "Last name is Suchar something-something-something. S-U-C-H-A-R-I-T-K-U-L. First name Decha."

The golden woman from my vision? "Doesn't ring a bell. Why do you think she was a client?"

"He. Had your card."

His interest was piqued. Not many people had his cards, despite Cordelia's efforts at spreading the word about Angel Investigations, preferably to "helpless people we can charge." Was this connected with what he had seen in the fire last night?

"Know anything about my new best friend Decha Sucharitkul?" Kate persisted. "Height five-ten, we're thinking. One hundred sixty, but all the fat was consumed. I've got people looking into his visa situation. How much you want to bet he was here illegally?"

If that was bait, he wasn't taking it.

"What was the cause of death?"

"That would help your memory?" she asked, obviously fishing. When he said nothing, she sighed. "Burn victim. Like I told you about. Weird stuff."

Then she delivered the zinger: "He was the body in the apartment fire last night, Angel. He's the one I mentioned to you."

Angel glanced at his computer. *Spontaneous human combustion,* he found himself thinking, in Doyle's voice.

He'd once seen a photo of a guy who had burst into flames. The guy had been sitting in an over-stuffed chair. He'd burned in half; when he'd been found, his legs were still upright. Both he and the chair had burned completely through from his waist up. His upper half and the back of the chair had been piles of ash.

He wondered if the woman in the blue fire was related to the dead man on his screen. Maybe she was his girlfriend. Or his sister.

She probably isn't even real, he reminded him-self. *I saw her through magickal means, not a video dating service.*

"Don't you find it amazingly coincidental that he was there and you were there, too?"

"What kind of ID did he have?" Angel queried.

"Believe it or not, the only other thing on him was a book with his name written inside it. *English as a Second Language*. Funny thing. Another burn vic-tim of mine was his English tutor. Her name was Olive LaSimone."

"How'd you get all that?" he asked.

"Now, Angel, you know I don't kiss and tell," she responded.

"I haven't got anything," Angel told her honestly. "I've never spoken to him."

"Have you spoken to other Asian immigrant types recently?" she asked. "I understand your other client of the night, Nira Surayanto, is Indonesian."

"Not that I'm aware of."

"Okay. Hold on." She covered the phone and talked to someone for a second.

"Sounds like I might have another one," she told him. "Let me know if you get anything on my guy, okay? Forensics says the poor bastard was sixteen at most if he was a hundred. Meanwhile, I gotta go visit another lovely crime scene. Let me know if you get anything."

"Sure." *Or not.*

They disconnected.

"Had to be Kate Lockley," Doyle said.

"We're leaving." Angel reached for his coat.

"To find Cordelia?"

Angel picked up his keys. Then he winced. The wound in his head from the serpent was stinging.

"You okay, man?" Doyle asked.

The phone rang. Angel picked up again.

"Yeah?"

"Angel? Oh, my God, it's Cordelia!" she shouted. "I'm in . . . where am I? I'm in a homeless shelter!"

"Cordelia, if you really need an advance on your salary . . ."

"Not that way in a homeless shelter," she interrupted. "Because the police brought me here!"

"The police?"

She huffed. "Will you just come down here? Something really weird is going on, and no way am I taking the bus."

"Okay. Give me the address."

"His card was in my purse!" Cordelia wailed.

"Stay calm." Angel had no idea what she was talking about.

"Calm? I had a date for a really rich guy's funeral!"

"Okay, Cordy. We're leaving now."

As she gave him the address, Doyle watched with obvious concern. Angel hung up and Doyle said, "What about the police?"

"We'll find out when we get there."

"But she's all right." Doyle frowned at him. "She *is* all right, right?"

"Let me put it this way. The thing she was most worried about was that she'd lost some guy's phone number."

"Oh." Doyle looked relieved. "*Oh.*" And hurt.

"I think he might have been dead," Angel added.

"Oh?" Doyle brightened. "Those things never work out. A girl like Cordy, a dead guy would bore her to tears."

Smiling faintly, Angel led the way out of the office and down the hall toward the covered car lot, where his convertible was parked. They got in and Angel peeled out.

Suddenly Doyle moaned. His demonic face—a

sort of blue Pinhead affair, with spiky things protruding everywhere—whipped into existence. The demon convulsed and shook wildly. Angel kept driving, knowing that Doyle was having a vision. There was nothing Angel could do but wait for it to run its course.

Doyle's human face reasserted itself as he exhaled, groaning as he did so.

"What did you see?" Angel asked.

"This one was bad," Doyle moaned.

"Painful?"

"To see, I mean." He grimaced. "It was a really lovely girl." Doyle frowned hard. "I guess you'd say a young woman. And she was burned, Angel. Like that autopsy photo on the computer screen."

"Was she dressed in gold clothes?"

Doyle looked at him curiously. "She was."

Angel hung a left. "I saw her, too. Last night."

Doyle was clearly startled. "You did? That's a new one."

"I saw her dancing."

"She was definitely burned in my vision. Not a pretty sight."

Then Doyle groaned and closed his eyes. "She's in a club," he said. "Club Ko-something. Didn't get it all."

Angel frowned. That was the way Doyle's visions were sometimes: rather vague and unfocused, but ultimately, always accurate. They were images of the people The Powers That Be wanted Angel to rescue.

A burning woman, he thought. *A vision Doyle and I shared.* That was something new.

And it felt like something big.

A police officer materialized after the screaming started. He went dashing off and Cordelia yelled at him about her purse, but had no idea if he heard her.

It was his partner, named Jason, who walked her to the shelter. He was on his police guy phone the whole time, rattling off numbers instead of words, so she had no idea what was going on.

After she called Angel, she took off her panty hose, washed her feet, and put her shoes on without the panty hose. Now she sat on a metal folding chair with a cup of coffee in her hand and a powdered-sugar doughnut on a paper napkin on her thigh. A man was facing her—not Mr. Change Guy, who had refused to come into the shelter—but someone just like him.

"I was just a kid when Pearl Harbor was attacked," an old man was telling her. "Kid like you. Now my son sells computers to the Japanese. Tell me about *that.*"

"Um," Cordelia said. "What would you like to know?"

"Says he's in love with the country. Wants to move to Tokyo." He wagged his finger at her. "Now, you tell me about *that*."

She scrunched her face at him. "Same question?" she repeated.

All of a sudden police cars came screeching to a halt in front of the plate-glass window of the shelter. Police officers were piling out and running past.

"Wow, what's going on?" she said, half-rising.

"Lotta crime," the man said. "What do you think about that?"

"I think you should relocate to someplace nicer," she said, watching the police. *That person I heard screaming must be . . . badly hurt.*

She crossed her fingers and hoped that that was all it was.

The men around her were oblivious. It was almost dinnertime, according to her Pearl Harbor friend, and that seemed to be the only thing on their addled minds.

She was unnerved. She kept thinking about her old boyfriend, Xander, okay, who had not been her boyfriend by the time she'd left Sunnydale. She'd always half-expected him to end up like one of these stinky old guys. But he was helping Buffy and Giles do the ghost-busting thing, and from what she'd heard, he was actually useful.

A Zeppo no longer, she thought, a bit wistfully.

The cops were still coming. And going. And talking into their walkie-phonie things. Cordelia was getting more and more nervous.

There was a stir among the men.

Goulash time, Cordelia guessed. *Mac and cheese. And I'm so hungry I'd eat it if they offered me any.*

And if they eat off paper plates.

But the stir was caused by the arrival of Angel and Doyle. Angel towered in the doorway, looking tall and good, but also very serious and take-charge. He had that air about him, like he could and would take care of your problems.

And preferably, charge you money, Cordelia thought as she waved. *After all, people spend hundreds of dollars on their pets. Angel saves people's lives.*

She stood. "Angel, over here!"

Her doughnut fell on the floor. Her new old friend divebombed for it and popped the entire thing in his mouth without even wiping it off.

"Ew," Cordelia said. Then, a little frantically, "Angel!"

The two men saw her this time and rushed over.

"Cordelia, what happened? What are you doing here?" Doyle demanded, all worries and frowns.

"I got mugged," she said breathlessly. "By two little kids and an old lady. She got mad at me because I wouldn't give her any change and then she and the little kids, who had already tried to steal my purse once, just took off with it."

She huffed. "Only, I guess it wasn't a mugging, because I didn't get hit."

"This is a terrible area," Doyle muttered.

"Then there was all this screaming." Cordelia sipped her coffee, even though it was still warm outside. The stiff Santa Ana winds were picking up, and the panes in the large windows overlooking the street rattled and shook.

"So my police officer friend, Jason, walked me over here and then went to check on it," she continued. "But by then it had stopped, and I don't know if he's coming back or what."

She sniffed. "Does that smell like steak to you? Because my friend, Mr. Sticky Floor Doughnut Guy, told me they're having macaroni and cheese for dinner."

She caught the look that passed between Doyle and Angel.

"We'll take a look around," Angel said. He turned to go back outside. Doyle trailed behind him.

"Oh, no," she protested, "don't leave me here."

Cordelia took a couple of steps. But minus her panty hose, her cheap shoes were rubbing on newly formed blisters. "Ouch!"

"Sit down. Drink your coffee," Angel ordered her. She watched them go.

"I don't eat meat. I'm a Libertarian," the stinky man informed her. His mouth was snowy with powdered sugar. "We're having macaroni and cheese."

"That's . . . whatever," she said. She limped back to her chair and sat down. Anxiously she looked over her shoulder, hoping Angel and Doyle would soon reappear.

The little girl who had helped steal her purse was staring at her through the window.

"Hey!" Cordelia cried. "Stop, thief!"

She hobbled toward the front door. The girl hesitated a moment, then dashed away. Cordelia's purse strap was slung over her shoulder, and she was so small that the purse itself was dragging on the ground behind her.

"Give that to me!" Cordelia shouted. "At least give me Jusef's business card!"

The girl threw her a terrified look and kept going.

It occurred to Cordelia that this could be a trap. But her stuff was involved, and she wasn't giving up her material possessions without a fight. She had so few of them these days. *Plus, Jusef's phone numbers are in there.*

"Angel! Doyle!" she yelled. "You guys!"

She limped down a different alley, distinguished only by the even more disgusting garbage on the ground, but no glass, thank goodness, and the smell of steak was even stronger. Burnt steak, in fact. But there was no way she was going to catch the little girl. All she heard was the clatter-clatter-clatter of her footfalls as she receded once more into the distance.

Cordelia ground her teeth in frustration as she lurched to a stop.

At that moment Doyle came flying around the corner to her left and said, "What's happening?"

"The little creep who took my purse just came back to taunt me," she said angrily. "Where were you guys? You don't have on cheap high heels. You could have caught her." She looked around the corner.

The alley was cordoned off with crime-scene tape. Two or three police officers stood guard in front of it while another one was quietly vomiting into a garbage can.

"What's going on?"

Doyle's face was pasty. "They found something, Cordy."

She stared at him in horror. "Not the little girl."

"No. A body. An adult." He held her arms as she moved to look around him. "You don't want to see this. Trust me."

Man, is Kate going to be pissed, Angel thought. *There's not going to be one square inch of ground those cops haven't walked over. Didn't they see* The Bone Collector?

While the police officers busied themselves with

contaminating the crime scene, Angel had managed to go around the large factory building on the corner and make his way up a rickety fire escape. From there he had jumped quietly and gracefully from one roof to the other. Now he watched from the roof of another building that stank of human waste. He hunkered down and listened carefully.

They had found a body. It had been a man. He was horribly burned. His name had been Ernesto Torres. In his pocket was a ring of keys, each numbered. Also, amazingly, a wad of parking tickets in a jacket he had been carrying in the warm evening. The police were guessing that he had dropped the jacket as soon as the burning had started, which was why the jacket had been spared.

Apparently Mr. Torres was fond of parking at a loading dock about five blocks south of his present location. Angel memorized the address.

It would be his next stop.

The coroner showed. And then Kate. As Angel had anticipated, Kate lost it when she saw how the cops had trampled the evidence. No need to listen carefully to what she had to say; he was sure people a block away could hear every syllable.

By the time he got back to the shelter, Doyle and Cordy were looking through her purse.

Good. Doyle found it, Angel thought approvingly.

When they both saw him, Cordy said, "What's going on?"

Angel shook his head at Doyle.

Doyle grimaced. "Let me look through your credit cards for you," he said to Cordy.

"What's happened?" Cordelia asked Angel. Then to Doyle, "I don't have any credit cards. I don't have any credit. Okay. I have one. I couldn't stand to cut it up. But it's expired."

With the precision of a gunslinger at high noon, she flipped open her wallet and pulled out a platinum American Express card.

"My glory days," she murmured.

She slipped it back in her wallet. Then she opened the coin purse. "My bus fare's still here. Oh, good! Here's Jusef's business card."

"The dead guy?" Angel asked.

"Trust me," Doyle said quickly. "You don't want to go out with a dead man. Despite all you might have heard, they're not good at small talk, and—"

She looked down at the card. "Angel, look."

Angel took the card. On the back, in an almost illegible scrawl in purple ink, were the words HELP US LADIEY. WE ARE KINDNAP. CELIA SUCHARITKUL.

The same name as Kate's second-to-most-recent burn victim.

"They were kidnapped?" Cordelia said. "Did you guys see them? We'll have to tell the police."

Angel turned the card back over. The name Jusef Rais was circled with the same purple ink.

"He's not dead?" Cordelia asked anxiously. "Because it was his father's funeral I got invited to—"

"*Oh,*" Doyle said. "So you're *not* dating a dead guy."

"Well, I hope not," Cordelia said waspishly. "I mean, I work for one, no offense, and I think that's enough dead guys in my life, don't you? Plus I think my manager must be dead, because he never gets me any acting jobs."

"Maybe that was him back there," Doyle suggested to Angel.

"No!" Cordelia wailed. "No! My dates only die in Sunnydale, okay? Not here, too!"

"Unless he was going under the alias of Ernesto Torres, your date's probably still alive," Angel assured her.

There was a sober moment. Cordelia looked a little pale. "So, there's a dead guy back there?"

"Yeah." Doyle looked a bit abashed.

Cordelia sighed. "I was hoping it was just something gross that you didn't want me to see," she said to Doyle. She gave him a weak smile. "Which I thought was kind of nice of you. But you know, back in Sunnydale, I saw all kinds of gross stuff and still managed to be pleasant and attractive."

"And the trend continues," Doyle offered.

She took the compliment, but Angel could see she was shaken. She gestured to the card again.

"So, do you think my date kidnapped those kids?"

"Maybe the little girl was trying to ask you to contact him," Doyle suggested. "Maybe he's related to her."

"We should check it out," Angel said. "You up for a funeral, Doyle?"

"Been to a few really good ones in my day," Doyle said.

Cordelia looked uncomfortable. "Um, you guys, I don't know if they have a list of guests or anything . . ."

"I was thinking we'd make our own way," Angel said.

"A little recon." Doyle nodded.

"We'll get you home. Then Doyle and I will get ready. Were you going to take a cab?"

"Jusef will send a limo," she said, lifting her chin. "I'm supposed to call."

"Okay." Angel looked down at his clothes. "We'd better change. See if we can blend in a little." He glanced at Cordelia. "Rich crowd?"

"They own a film studio in Indonesia."

Doyle looked crestfallen.

"When are you supposed to call?"

"Three hours from when we met. . . ." She glanced at Doyle's watch. "Oh, no, in an hour and a half! I have to change! My hair!" She grabbed her head. "I'm a mess!"

Doyle and Angel exchanged another look.

"What?" Cordelia demanded.

"Saving the world," Doyle drawled. "It's not just a job. It's an adventure."

Then footsteps sounded behind them, and Angel said, "How much you want to bet Kate wants to know what we're doing here?"

He would not have lost.

CHAPTER SIX

"Well, well, if it isn't the Caped Crusader," Kate said dryly as she walked up to Angel, Doyle, and Cordy. "And you just happened to be in the neighborhood of my brand-new homicide."

"It's not because of that," Cordelia cut in. "These little kids stole my purse. Who, apparently, have been kidnapped. Or maybe they're just playing a trick. And I got change from a crazed man with an extreme body odor problem to call Angel to come get me."

Cordelia looked around. "There's a nice police officer named Jason who'll back me up. Who is single," she added, in case Kate was, too.

"Kidnapped?" Kate echoed.

Silently Angel handed her Jusef's card.

"Hey," Cordelia protested.

Kate looked at her sharply.

"May I copy down the number?" Cordy asked in a small voice.

Kate studied the card. She flipped it over a couple times. "Do you know Jusef Rais?" she asked Cordelia.

"I'm going to his father's funeral. I hope," she added, glancing at the card.

"Let's start at the top." Kate waited expectantly.

"Okay. These two kids scoped me out," she said.

She began to tell her story. Without realizing it, Angel started tuning her out. The wound in his head was stinging. He felt as if his brains were turning to ice, if such a thing were possible.

Doyle scrutinized him. "What's wrong?" he asked quietly.

Angel said, "Something bit me. We'd better do a little research when we get back to my place."

Doyle cocked his head. "Something . . . that was not a dog or a cat?"

Angel nodded. "Definitely not a cat."

"And so, then she must have written this on the card," Cordelia was finishing up.

Kate looked askance at Angel. "Looks like the mountain came to Muhammad."

When he didn't say anything, she pressed, "You were supposed to come down to the station to make a statement on the apartment guy. And now you're here for this guy. And meanwhile, we've got a possible kidnapping involving someone your secretary's going on a date with."

"To a funeral," Cordelia amended. "Not exactly a date."

Kate ignored her. "By the time you actually get down to my place of business, it's not going to be a statement, it's going to be a book."

"Wouldn't fly in a novel," he replied. "Too many coincidences."

"Ma'am." A police officer approached Kate cautiously. "We need to deal with the evidential chain of custody."

Kate made a comment Angel figured was unprintable.

"Don't go anywhere," she said to the three. She looked at Cordelia and Doyle. "Any of you."

Cordelia frowned and raised her hand slightly. "But I have to wash my—"

"Yes?" Kate snapped.

Cordelia's shoulders drooped. "Nothing," she said weakly. "This has so not been my day."

Looking sympathetic, Doyle stepped toward Cordelia. Kate glared at him. He froze in his tracks.

"Not moving," he assured her, half-raising his hands. "Didn't get the part?" he asked Cordy.

"Doubtful." She added plaintively, "I didn't ask to be robbed near a crime scene, okay?"

Kate stomped off.

"Whew," Doyle drawled. "That one is tightly wound."

Angel watched her go. "She's got a lot on her plate."

"Those homeless guys are having macaroni and cheese tonight," Cordelia announced. "And for the record? I swear she was in an episode of *Charmed*."

When you're rich, you can do a lot of really cool things, Jusef thought.

For instance, you can get other people to do a lot of really evil things.

The short-haired elderly lady had been brought to the compound, there to beg for her life and turn over her partner in crime. One of Jusef's Brethren, attempting to move Ernesto Torres's body before it was discovered, had discovered the children running in panic down an alley. He had caught the boy, though the girl had gone free.

The boy had told him about the old lady, and they'd picked her up on the way back.

It seemed that she had been teaching some of her little charges at the sweatshop how to pick pockets. Petty crime like that was expressly forbidden by the Rais family. There was no need to call attention to themselves in such a tawdry and unnecessary way.

But the woman had been desperate to pay off her passage to America. It seemed that her daughter back in Bangkok was very ill, and not expected to live much longer. All she wanted from life was to see her one last time. She herself had been a street child, stealing wallets and jewelry so she could survive.

When Chairman Mao had risen to power in China, this misguided being had become a social activist in Thailand. For that, she had been hounded and sent to prison. There, she had developed a fascination for the land of America, a brutal country that nevertheless offered freedom of thought and independence.

Years later one of her fellow inmates in the prison had run into her on the street. He had offered to help her get to America.

If only she'd realized it was a ploy to put her to work as a slave. She became a despicable collaborator, forcing young children to work until they dropped. She couldn't stand to see them suffer so.

So she had put some of the children to work in minor thievery, extracting a portion of their takings in return for excusing them from their work in the sweatshop. She forged records, penciling in their hours and lying about how many garments were sewn in the shop.

All this she had confessed to, in hopes of mercy. She even offered to turn over all her profits from her illegal venture.

She had no knowledge of any demons fighting on the wrong side, however.

Her death had been slow and very miserable.

Now the torches in the Temple of Latura cast shadows on the face of the little boy who trembled before Jusef. Haggard and exhausted, he looked like a little old man . . . but he would never live long enough to be old or a man.

The great wheel of karma is definitely turning in my favor, Jusef thought.

The little boy's name was Kliwon Sucharitkul, the younger brother of that fool, Decha. Decha, originally a follower, had turned traitor. He'd lost his nerve and tried to abandon the work. He'd been a fool. Latura was not a god who allowed betrayal.

Kliwon's pencil-thin wrists were chained to the wall. Tears flooded his yellow-brown face and dampened his blue batik shirt. Jusef had never seen anyone cry so hard. It was eerie how the child could weep so, yet never make a sound. Also, quite fascinating.

Hooded and robed, Jusef stood before the boy and said, in Bahasa Indonesia, "You do understand why I'm angry, don't you?"

Kliwon lowered his head. Jusef sighed. Beneath his hood, he clicked his teeth thoughtfully. Had he himself ever been that humble? Doubtful. His father used to laugh and tell him he was born proud and ambitious.

From a tyrant like his father, that was high praise

indeed. But no praise had ever come from those lips after Jusef told Bang he wanted to be a musician.

That is, until Jusef began his search into the mysteries of the occult. Then his father was his friend again.

Oh, yes. For a little while, anyway.

He remembered it now: the last day he had cared what his father thought. The day he had become his own man.

Latura's man.

And one of the strangest nights of his life.

Paris, 1996

There was a man, or a creature. Jusef wasn't certain which.

But this man could not be killed.

Jusef had discovered all this quite by accident. Jamming with a group one night down in Montmartre, he had staggered down the street toward the nearest Metro stop.

He'd turned right onto Rue Mariotte, strolling along, even though it was three in the morning. He had no bodyguards with him. They cramped his style.

And then he heard the fighting. And the growling.

Dim lights overhead obscured his vision, but what he saw mesmerized him: a tall creature shaped like a man, but wearing a demonic face. His hair was dark, his skin pale. He wore a long black coat.

He was fighting something very like himself, something with grotesque features and long, sharp teeth. Their strength was incredible; as they slammed into each other, they went flying and crashing against the brick walls of the alley.

The other creature kept snarling and attacking, but it was obvious to Jusef that the tall one was going to win. The amount of abuse both were taking was staggering. Normal men would have been killed by now.

And then, suddenly, the tall one did something to the other one. Thrust a stick into him, or a magic wand. And the other one exploded into dust.

Jusef felt as though he had turned to stone. He was completely paralyzed with amazement.

The victor turned and raced down the alley, swallowed up by the night.

It was over.

Jusef began the quest for such power. He hired researchers, mediums, *dukun,* and fortune-tellers. He bought expensive volumes of occult lore.

He began to make discoveries. Wonderful discoveries. He used them to push his singing career forward.

His father, who had spies everywhere, heard of it, of course. He usurped Jusef's hopes and dreams. Almost worse, he brought in Jusef's moronic cousin,

Slamet. Jusef did not understand his father's high opinion of Slamet, who lacked intelligence and ambition, not necessarily in that order.

Father, son, and nephew became skilled in their use of magick. Bang rose to even greater heights in Indonesian power circles. World leaders in the know began to curry his favor. American generals joked about getting "More Bang for your buck."

After a time Jusef understood his father's unspoken bargain: His son might use a few tricks here and there to further his career, but the real power must fuel Bang's ambitions. It was the only way he would spare Jusef from the unwanted mantel as heir to his legacy.

Jusef made more discoveries; and then the ultimate discovery: how to live forever.

Latura was the God of the Dead. And if you served him, you could live forever. Bang made it clear that if immortality were granted to anyone in their family, it would be himself.

But how could he trust me to hand over the secret to eternal life, if just one of us could have it? Jusef wondered.

The answer: He never had. Not if he could move in strange circles of glowing blue light. He had never shared *that* with his son. And the demon who escaped him, what of that? What had his father fought the last night of his life?

Jusef wondered how Slamet was feeling now,

with Bang dead. The gods were supposed to have protected Bang Rais from all harm. Jusef's father and Slamet had made many vows, sacrificed hundreds of no-accounts here and in Indonesia, to keep Bang safe from disease and injury. That included assassination attempts, which were numerous. And their efforts had been rewarded.

But the three of them had only sketchy knowledge about Latura, based upon some pages in the diary of an eighteenth-century Catholic priest. While they had managed to channel Latura's power, they had not been able to contact the god himself.

Then Jusef learned something wonderful: There was a Book, a written record of all the knowledge necessary to bring Latura into this world. That was the dread lord's price for the gift of eternal life. But it could be granted only to one person at a time— someone who would perform sacrifices, learn the rites and incantations, and provide Latura with a properly prepared vessel in which to walk the earth. All this would be explained in the Book.

Jusef became fairly certain that the Book was in a little church near Nias.

He sent men out to search for it. That was also when Jusef took the risk and began systematically lying to his father.

He formed the Brethren of Latura, a super-secret cult of acolytes. He wondered if Bang had learned of them, too, the same as he had learned about the lying.

No matter. He's worm meat, he told himself nervously.

Then he had learned that the Book had been smuggled to America. Someone had had the brilliant notion of disguising it as a textbook. Some wonderful joke. *English as a Second Language.* Jusef had begun tracking down the possessors of such a book.

Interesting that they all belonged to the same Catholic parish in Los Angeles.

And that the parish priest was from Indonesia.

And that he had gone into hiding about the same time that Jusef had learned all this information.

And I'm going to find that damn Book, if I have to kill everyone in Los Angeles to do it.

Speaking of killing . . .

"You weren't trying to steal from that young lady, were you?"

The boy made no answer. Instead he hung his head and cried even harder.

Jusef waited. And waited. If he had learned anything in his years of being the son of Bang Rais, it was that he who made the first move always lost.

Jusef gestured toward the darkness. The flapping of wings echoed against the smoky, blood-drenched walls. The click of talons chittered a fraction louder on the slick, wet floor.

The boy struggled frantically and said, "No. No, *pak*."

"Only your sister. And you tried to punish her for it." The old woman had told him that before she died, in hopes that he would spare the boy.

"She didn't. I wasn't . . . I didn't hit her to punish her. She said I was stupid. That's why."

The boy stared up at him. Just to be impish, Jusef stepped farther back into the shadows, making himself into a specter.

"Please, *pak*." The gibbering child broke into a native dialect, guttural and unpleasant. It was something about his mother, and how heartbroken she would be if her children died. How the authorities would look for them.

"You little slave," Jusef said derisively. "Do you think your pleas will move me? Jusef of Latura? How you underestimate his power!"

The boy kept begging, kept pleading. His sobs were noisy now.

Far too noisy. Jusef looked up, thinking of the many people aboveground, guests strolling through the compound. He looked back at the boy, who was flinging himself forward, cutting the skin on his little wrists to ribbons. Blood droplets went flying.

The talons skittered eagerly across the concrete.

"Where's my sister?" the boy shouted. "What have you done with my sister?"

Jusef regarded the child almost kindly. "That was to be my next question," he told the boy. "Since you clearly don't know where she is, you have just signed your own death certificate."

The demon—Jusef's demon—scrabbled into the light from the overhanging bulb. Four-legged, its skin a shiny green with thick, deep facial features carved deeply into its crimson flesh, its wings fluttered as fast as a hummingbird. With a shriek of fierce excitement, it launched itself at Kliwon.

"I know who has the Book!" the boy shouted.

Jusef was astounded.

"Stop!" he commanded the demon.

But it was too late. Its wide-open mouth engulfed the boy's face. There were a few whimpers, indicating that the child was still alive, but it really was too late.

Jusef sat slowly down on the floor and listened in darkness to the slurping and the crunching. He looked at the altar to his god and murmured, "For you, my dark lord. Another sacrifice."

His sister, he thought. *Celia*.

Priority.

Jusef was calm and collected when he ascended the temple and joined his cousin in the receiving line. The *sedhekah* would begin soon. The more general reception had already begun.

Jusef saw Slamet at the entrance to the palatial

family home. It was a monument to Art Deco, written up in dozens of magazines. The clean lines were delicately detailed with mauve and lavender neon, highlighting a fantastic crystal sculpture of Diana with her bow centered in a full moon above the double doors. Glass bricks glowed warmly with candlelight. Though the body of Bang Rais lay in the ground, an altar had been set up in the living room as a memorial. Guests were invited—translation: expected—to pay their respects to the gods and to the spirit of the dear departed.

In a beautifully cut black suit, Slamet looked every inch the grieving favorite nephew of a very wealthy man. Jusef wore black as well, very cutting-edge Italian, with a collarless white shirt and no tie. Black cowboy boots. He noted Slamet's look of disapproval and grinned to himself. *What a tiny-minded man my cousin is,* he thought.

Then a police car glided through the entrance gates. Slamet raised his brows in alarm and glanced at Jusef.

"Now what?"

Jusef shrugged. "I don't have the slightest idea."

"Those deaths," Slamet whispered. "They cannot be traced?"

Jusef rolled his eyes. "Are we going to start this again?"

"Why didn't you just kill them in a less obvious

way?" Slamet continued. "Or take them somewhere else to kill them?"

"I was flushing out our enemies," Jusef informed him. "Letting them know we had the power. Making them think we have the knowledge."

"But they know we don't have the Book," Slamet said quietly.

"How? How do they know that? Hell, for all they know, there are two Books. Twenty. It's all ancient lore mixed in with legend, Slamet. Do you know how many 'true crosses' there were in Europe during the Crusades?"

A beautiful Indian somberly approached. Jusef silently bowed. She bowed soberly back. She was, or had been, highly placed in the Indian government. Jusef couldn't remember who on earth she was.

"Madame Krishnamurti," Slamet said respectfully. "Thank you for attending our reception."

"Madame," Jusef echoed. "Thank you."

"My sympathies on the death of a great man," she told them.

Then she swept past.

The police car approached. Slamet said, "What is this? In front of everyone? On the night of Uncle's funeral!"

"It wouldn't happen in Indonesia," Jusef agreed.

The passenger door opened and a blond woman

stepped out. She looked familiar. Of course. She'd been on the news, talking about the burnings.

Talking to Meg.

"Mr. Rais?" she queried.

I'll let Slamet handle this, he thought. He remained silent.

"Jusef Rais?" she continued.

His heart skipped a beat, but he managed to retain his composure.

She flipped open a leather wallet and flashed a badge. "I'm Detective Lockley of the L.A.P.D. I've got to ask you a few questions."

"We're in the middle of my father's death observances," he said. "May I help you another time?"

"Sorry." She made a moue of apology, but it was clear she didn't give a damn who had died or what was going on.

"Let's go into a private area," Jusef suggested.

Slamet turned to follow. The woman held up a hand.

"Just your brother for the moment," she informed him.

"He's my cousin," Slamet said. He frowned. "Jusef, shall I call our lawyer?"

"You anticipate trouble?" the detective asked smoothly.

Slamet actually flushed. Jusef wanted to strangle him right then and there.

"No, no," Slamet said quickly, making a lie of his own words. "It's just that we're very rich, you see, and very well-known. We need to be conscious of our place in the community."

"I see." She shrugged. "You call whoever you need to call, Mr. Rais. I just want to ask your cousin some questions."

Slamet stomped away, clearly angered. Jusef decided to act reasonable. He smiled and said, "I assume since you're on duty, you can't have champagne."

"Nothing for me, thank you," she said with asperity.

Jusef didn't want to push it, so he led her into the house. They walked past a number of servants wearing black mourning bands around their left arms, and into a sitting room his mother had always liked. She had died four years before, and Jusef still missed her.

"Nice," the detective said, seating herself in a wicker chair with a balloon-shaped back. Frangipangi surrounded her.

Jusef sat opposite her. He crossed his legs and folded his hands.

"A little girl stole the purse of a friend of yours tonight," the detective began. "Her name was Celia Sucharitkul."

Jusef couldn't help his jerk of recognition. He saw that she noted it, and tried to look worried.

"She's run away, I'm afraid," he told her, leaning forward slightly. "She had some kind of fight with her brothers."

"They are . . . ?"

He thought a moment. *What had the little one been named?*

"Kliwon," he said. "And Decha."

"Decha was found dead."

He sat up. "What?"

"Burned to death. We've found a number of homicides like that throughout the city. Would you know anything about that, Mr. Rais?"

"No. Of course not."

Meg, who had seen Jusef and started walking toward him, stood quietly, listening. Her heart was pounding.

They've come for me, she thought. *They think I'm connected in some way.*

In her mind's eye, she saw Olive's disfigured body. Her stomach roiled and she wanted to be sick.

Then just as vividly, the face of a man filled her field of vision. He was extremely pale, and his eyes and hair were dark. He looked puzzled.

He looked as if he could see her.

Was he an angel?

"Angel?" she whispered. "Can you help me?"

     ❖   ❖   ❖

Angel was tamping white sage and rosemary into what looked like a tea ball. He waited a beat and then said, "Yes, Doyle?"

Doyle cricked his neck as he looked up from a massive old leather book. "Yeah, man?"

Angel frowned slightly. "Didn't you just say my name?"

Doyle shook his head. "No." He looked at Angel again. "Isn't that the second time that's happened?"

"Yes." Angel touched the bite on his head. "I remember once back in Sunnydale, Buffy got some demon's blood on her. She could hear people's thoughts."

"Telepathy," Doyle identified helpfully.

Angel put down the talisman he was concocting and paged through the book he'd gotten the recipe from. It was a translation called *The Demonic Compendium*, and it contained some information about Asian demons.

"I'm connecting with someone, and I don't know who it is." He turned another page. "If you ever see this in the original Latin on eBay, let me know. I never trust translations."

"That's a rare one, that," Doyle said, indicating the book. "Only a couple copies in existence."

I won't remember, a voice whispered.

Angel blinked. "I heard it distinctly that time. It's a woman's voice. She sounds young. And frightened."

They looked at each other. "Maybe it's the woman in the vision we shared," Angel said.

Doyle held up the sketch Angel had made. They'd drawn it together, both studying it. They'd come up with the fact that her clothes were Javanese, and her dance pose was Balinese.

Indonesian.

Rais was an Indonesian name. A few minutes on the Net, and Angel learned that the Raises were a very wealthy and influential family, both in the U.S. and Asia. Their primary source of wealth was the garment industry.

"Limo's almost here," Cordelia called. "The driver just called my cell phone to let me know."

They had brought her back to Angel's place so they could work on the mystery of the burnings. None too pleased to be rushed, she nevertheless understood the why of it.

"Okay. Party time," Angel said.

He and Doyle were dressed in black suits. The night was warm, so no duster. They took the elevator up and met Cordy in the office, who was pacing a little.

Doyle's eyes widened at the sight of Cordelia.

"You look great," he said with admiration.

She did. Hair pulled back in a chignon, a few wisps around her face, her black dress was low cut without being inappropriate. She had on a jet choker and matching bracelet, black stockings, and black high heels.

"You guys aren't bad, either," she said.

"Here." Angel held out a small cloisonné ball.

Cordelia made a face. "Ew. What's that for? It stinks."

"It's a talisman," Angel said. "It should help to ward off evil, if my reference can be trusted. I really need the original Latin."

"Did you try shopping.com?" Cordelia queried. "I spend half the day—of my lunch *hour*—there. They've got all kinds of great stuff. That I can no longer afford."

"Better times are coming," Doyle assured her.

"Put it in your purse," Angel told her.

"I really don't want to." She shivered theatrically. "I spent a number of hours among the hygienically challenged, and I just sprayed myself with about twenty dollars' worth of very expensive perfume. Plus this is my good purse, for nighttime, and I can't afford to get another one if it stays stinky."

Angel continued to hold it out. "Would you rather burn to a cinder?"

"Do it," Doyle urged. He looked at Angel. "Where's mine?"

"I made three." Angel gestured to his desk, where the other two sat.

He handed one to Doyle and kept the other, sliding it into the pocket of his suit.

"Okay. Doyle, stick close to Cordy. I'll follow close behind," Angel said. "If they boot you, Doyle, they probably won't let me in, either."

He looked at Cordelia. "And if we can't get in, what do you do?"

"Pitch a fit," she announced, "which I am good at doing. As you know."

"As I know," Angel concurred.

"You could also say you're not feeling well," Doyle suggested.

"Whatever it takes," Angel said. "Just get the hell out of there. You're not going in without at least one of us."

"Okay." She shifted her shoulders. "Are you sure you don't want me to wear a wire? Or a wig? Or have a fakey-sounding foreign accent like Doyle's?"

"Cordy, you're getting way too into this," Angel warned. "Throttle back, okay?"

"And for your information, my accent is not 'fakey-sounding,'" Doyle said, miffed. "I was born with this accent."

"Well, Angel's Irish and he doesn't run around imitating a leprechaun."

"He's been gone from the home county a wee bit longer than I have, too."

"Okay, okay. Don't get all wound up," Cordelia lectured him. "We need you frosty for the mission."

Angel peered at her. "What have you been auditioning for lately?"

"Mouthwash."

Doyle crossed to the window and peered through the venetian blinds. "Limo just pulled up."

"Here we go," Cordelia whispered.

"Nervous?" Doyle asked.

Cordelia snorted. "Yeah, right. The Queen of Cool is nervous just because she's riding in a limo to a rich family's compound for a funeral. Please."

"Take deep breaths," Doyle suggested.

She rolled her eyes and said, "C'mon, let's go. I'm hoping they have a buffet, because I'm starving."

Doyle and Cordelia left together. Angel stayed in the hallway to give them a head start.

The driver got out and opened the door. As his two passengers passed him, he gave Cordelia a strange look, moving his gaze to her purse. He looked left, then right, maybe gave someone in the shadows a brief shake of his head. Angel couldn't tell for certain.

But I have a bad feeling about this.

It was an actual physical sensation that began in the painful snakebite on the crown of his head and shot straight down into his toes.

Angel crossed to the front door, opened it, and stepped into the night.

CHAPTER SEVEN

As Angel headed for the covered parking garage where he kept his vehicle, he was certain he heard footsteps trailing him. He did the old trick of speeding up and slowing down; whoever was shadowing him was either really good or a figment of his imagination.

Make that door number one, he thought as something very hard came down very fast across his shoulders.

He doubled forward and executed a snap-kick directly backward, slamming into the midsection of his attacker. Without a moment's hesitation, he turned ninety degrees and planted a sidekick in the same location.

His attacker was dressed in black clothing. He had long black hair pulled back in a ponytail and a wicked-ugly scar down the left side of his face. A tattoo of a death's head had been worked into the scar tissue, and as the man winced in pain, the tattoo seemed to contort and spasm.

Angel turned another ninety degrees and pushed the man backward. He advanced on him, pushing again.

"Who are you?" he demanded. "Who sent you?"

The man coughed blood. He tried to shield his face as Angel rammed a fist directly into his nose.

Bellowing, he dropped to his knees. His head flopped forward. The man braced himself with his hands, panting.

Angel slammed his foot down on the man's right hand. With a shriek, the man threw himself backward.

Angel bent down and grabbed him by the collar. "Who sent you?"

"I serve Latura," the man croaked. Blood dribbled down his chin.

"Who's that?"

The man spit out a tooth. His eyes widened. He said, "Kill me now, or my master will."

"Maybe I'll let your master," Angel said.

"No," the man begged. "He will let Latura eat my soul."

"Latura being your martial arts instructor?"

The man's eyes widened. His gaze ticked to a point behind Angel. Angel had seen that look before, and he knew what to do.

He dropped to the ground and rolled out of the way as a second attacker launched himself at him.

With nothing to stop his trajectory, Angel's assailant arced into the air, then unceremoniously crashed on top of the first attacker. Both let out roars of pain and frustration.

Before the second guy had time to realize what had hit him—or, more correctly, what he had hit—Angel was at his side, deftly twisting his arm.

"One more inch, and it'll snap," Angel promised him.

The man groaned. "Please, no. Latura, I serve you."

Angel frowned. "Does your boss have an address?"

The man remained silent. Then he shouted in pain as Angel made good on his threat to break his arm. The sound echoed in Angel's memory.

There was a time when I did things like this for pleasure, he thought. *I enjoyed hurting people.*

Now, I just need to get the job done.

Tears ran down the man's face. He murmured something, but Angel couldn't understand him.

"I will hurt you some more if I need to," Angel said in English. "Tell me who Latura is."

"My god," the man whispered.

"I'll ask one more time."

"My god. He is my god."

Ah.

"And you attacked me because?"

The man could barely speak now. "We are . . . to guard the family. I . . . I don't know why I was told to attack you."

"Who told you to?"

"Mustafa. The chauffeur."

"Of the limo?" Angel asked with alarm.

The man nodded, then he began to cry.

Angel whipped out a cell phone and punched in Cordelia's number. He waited while it rang.

And rang.

And rang.

A figure in the darkness melted back into the shadows. *Jusef is not going to like this*

"Are we in a movie or what?" Cordelia whispered excitedly to Doyle.

"What movie, *Big Trouble in Little China?*" Doyle muttered.

They had made it past Checkpoint Charlie, or whatever passed for it in Indonesian circles. Now massive, jade-colored gates were taking their dear, sweet time opening, and Doyle was not loving the scene laid out before them.

Nor was he loving the fact that he had lost sight of Angel's convertible in the hubbub, the crush and density of which reminded him of trying to cross the border from Tijuana into San Diego at seven o'clock of a weekday morning, when all the maids, nannies, and gardeners commuted to their places of employment.

"It's just so . . ." She was at a loss for words, and no wonder. There were lanterns and torches and Chinese gongs and huge statues of weird mythical creatures that looked to be part alligator, part snake, and part icky demon thing. There were life-size topiaries of monkeys and elephants lit up with dozens of little white lights. Swirling masses of people in suits and evening gowns strolled around, carrying crystal glasses and looking very, very rich.

On their right, valets in black trousers and white shirts were parking more Beemers, Jags, and Mercedes than could be found at most dealerships. There went a classic T-bird. *Oh, God, and a Lotus.*

"Wow, this is some funeral," Cordelia murmured.

"It is grand," Doyle conceded. He turned around again.

"Relax," Cordelia whispered. "My phone hasn't gone off. So he's somewhere."

That didn't appease Doyle at all. It was not a foolproof plan, and he and Angel had both recognized that. Better, maybe, if he phoned if he did get onto the property. Phone batteries could get low, or reception jammed—all kinds of things. This way, they couldn't be positive that he'd made it.

The car slowed to a standstill. The door swept open.

"Hi," Cordelia said breathily. Her eyes gleamed as she took a male hand and climbed gracefully out of the limo. It was fairly probable the movie uppermost in her mind was *How to Marry a Millionaire*.

Doyle climbed out by himself, to find Cordelia facing a good-looking gent in a hip version of a business suit. When he saw Doyle he looked none too pleased, but Doyle didn't react. He didn't care.

"Selamat malam," the guy said. Then to Doyle, as if he was the only one in need of a translation, "Good evening."

"Same to you," Cordelia replied, but Doyle could tell she was disappointed about something. "Doyle, this is Slamet Rais. Slamet, my friend, Doyle."

"Ah, you brought a date." Slamet sounded hurt.

Cordelia smiled. "No. Just a friend." She added coyly, "Your cousin said the more people who came, the more honor your uncle would receive."

"So he did." Slamet held out his hand to Doyle. "Welcome."

As Doyle shook with the man, Cordelia looked back into the surge of people and vehicles gliding to a stop. The man—Slamet Rais—asked pleasantly, "Looking for someone?"

He knows something's up, Doyle realized. *Maybe he can detect the talismans.*

Doyle reached for Cordy. "I think we'd better go—"

But just at that moment, another man joined Slamet. A really big, tall man.

And another.

And a couple more.

"Please, the *sedhekah* is about to begin," Slamet said, pressing his palms together and making a little bow.

"Oh, good," Cordelia said, oblivious to the warning glances Doyle was trying to send her way.

In a little clump, everyone began to walk.

"Okay, so on to Ernesto Torres," the blond detective said to Jusef. "He was an employee of yours?"

"No, no," Jusef replied, sounding amused. "We rented factory space from him. I believe there were some code violations, but two months later the building inspector reported that everything had been put right. We have the records, if you would care to see them."

That's not true, Meg thought. *Ernesto Torres supervised a sewing crew.*

Abruptly the detective said, "May I please see the death certificate for your father?"

Meg gasped.

"Detective," Jusef said. "We have dealings all over the Pacific Rim, but my family is Indonesian. We practice *adat*, meaning that we keep to our customs. Our beliefs stipulate that the family takes personal care of the rituals associated with death. We do not hire outsiders, as you do. Preparation of the body, arranging the funeral pyre, is all done by the deceased's relatives."

"What does that have to do with his death certificate?" she demanded.

Meg was even more shocked. In Indonesia, one did not speak so disrespectfully to a Rais.

"I only meant to point out that we have our own physician as well. It was he who prepared the death certificate. My father's body never left the compound after he died." His voice rose slightly.

He's getting angry, Meg thought.

"So if for some reason you don't trust us . . ."

"Did you know Mr. Torres's body had been moved?" she switched.

There was a pause. Then Jusef said, "No, I didn't know that, Detective. How would I?"

"Apparently he was killed inside a warehouse." She looked down at a notepad in her lap. "And moved about seven blocks to a more public location. As if someone wanted him to be found."

Jusef shrugged. "I can't imagine why."

"Perhaps someone wanted to leave a warning."

"That could be," he allowed.

"Or maybe someone wanted him to be found by us."

"Also a possibility. Detective, I don't mean to be rude, but we have a custom called a *sedhekah*. It's supposed to start. I'm the son of the family, and I need to be there."

"All right." She flipped the notebook shut and picked up a black leather purse. Meg moved farther back into the shadows. "Again, Mr. Rais, I'm sorry for your loss."

"Thanks."

They both stood. The woman held out her hand. Jusef took it, and they shook.

"I'll see myself out," she told him.

He said nothing.

As soon as the detective left the sitting room, Meg lost her composure. She stumbled toward Jusef, who looked very startled.

"Baby," he said. He held out his arms.

"I'm scared," she murmured. "I'm connected to all this. I just don't know how."

He pulled her against his chest and stroked her hair. Then he walked her to one of the chairs and sat her down. He crouched in front of her and took her hands.

"Look into my eyes, Meg," he said.

She obeyed.

"Keep looking. See yourself as you are. The Meg I love."

Her smile was brief.

"See the beautiful woman I love. See her from head to toe."

She began to relax. The muscles in her back and shoulders loosened. Her head was heavy. It was hypnosis. They'd done this a hundred times, and each time it got easier to go under.

"You're a vessel of pure light," he said softly. "A perfect vessel. Say it after me, Meg."

"A vessel," she whispered.

"Yes. Each moment of your life. Each day of your life. The great wheel has turned to bring you to this."

"Yes," she said.

"Close your eyes now. See the flame in the eye."

It was a trick he had taught her, to help her fall into a hypnotic state. She was to envision a statue, and in the empty eye sockets of the statue, a flame. And in the flame, herself, dancing.

From head to toe, she was swathed in gold. She danced the *barong*; and her costume was of pure gold.

She was a temple dancer. She had always been a temple dancer, gliding through time. Her hands, her feet, making gestures that would bring the gods forth.

Bring the god forth.

Her hands said, *Latura*. Her feet, *Latura*.

Nias, Indonesia, 1863

The Servant quaked as the heads were brought. Shriveling as they dried, the faces looked inhuman.

The pots were brimming with the meat of the dead.

The headman, who had claimed her for his family, looked on approvingly as his sons' slaves brought more heads, and more. Could there be anyone left alive, besides this clan?

"My house does you great honor," the headman said to her. "Now you will marry my son. Now you will give him your magick."

The bridegroom was younger than she. He was strong, and virile. He and his raiding party had taken more heads in a single attack than any before, ever.

In their world, brides were bought with heads.

She had never seen so much death. With each rotting head flung at her feet, she closed her eyes and chanted, *For you, Latura, God of the Underworld.*

She did not want to be the cause of such slaughter. But what was she, if not the harbinger of death?

When the god walks among the living, he will destroy everything he touches. Everything he looks at. Everything he breathes on.

Of that she was certain. The knowledge was in her blood.

Suddenly she flung herself in front of the proud

young man. She gathered up her hair and exposed the back of her neck.

"Behead me," she begged, "rather than marry me."

There was a moment when no one moved and no one spoke. No one breathed.

Then something came down on her head, swift and sure, and she collapsed from the force of the blow.

No, I don't want to die, she thought desperately.

She didn't know then that no one ever really wants to die.

They want the pain to go away. The terror of the moment to subside.

But death?

Never.

When she woke up, she was in the home of the headman's family. Her bridegroom was with her, giving her a child.

Their daughter was born the following summer, and the Servant's blood flowed in her veins.

The Servant wept for her child's fate.

This time, she tried to strike a bargain with the god:

"If I write down all I know, will you spare her?"

In her blood, the god agreed. He promised that her daughter would live a good, if short, life, and that he would grant her safe passage to the home of his twin, Lowalangi, in the sky.

In return, the Servant, who had learned the ways

of the headhunters, scratched his incantations into bamboo rods. It took her months. She kept them hidden among her belongings.

When she was finished, the god caused a great fire that swept through the village. The only things that were spared were the bamboo rods.

And the child of the Servant, who lay shrieking among the charred ruins until a group of Dutch missionaries arrived, and found her.

They couldn't decipher the rods, nor did they care to. But a kindly nun, figuring that they might contain information about the child's heritage, lovingly gathered them up and carried them to their camp, placing them beside the sleeping baby, who was called Maria.

Slamet was entertaining Cordy and Doyle, but it was clear he had a lot on his mind.

He kept touching her, and it was starting to bother her. He'd touched a dead person recently. Well, no big. She was sure her touching-dead-people days weren't behind her. Especially if you included hugging Angel.

"So this washing dead people. It's an Indonesian thing," she continued, mostly to have something to say. She realized she hadn't eaten since breakfast— too nervous at the audition—and her stomach rumbled. She laughed to cover it, and he gave her an odd look.

"I can see why your own words amuse you," he replied. "Seeing as how my country is fourteen thousand islands." He held out his hands. "There really isn't much that's 'Indonesian.' Perhaps if you count Bahasa Indonesia, our primary language. But even it is not Indonesian. It's Malay."

"Oh, yes," she said brightly. She kept wondering where the heck on a map she'd ever seen fourteen thousand islands.

Slamet, Doyle, and she strolled beneath strings of Chinese lanterns of red and yellow, past a long, white linen table attended by men in tuxes. They were pouring flutes of champagne as quickly as waiters with large, brass trays were lining up to get them.

"We're not Muslim," Slamet said. At the merest glance from him, a waiter scurried up with two fresh glasses perched delicately on a small gold lacquer square. Slamet took them both and handed one to Cordelia, and one to Doyle.

"To karma," he said, "the great turning of the wheel."

"Same to you," Cordelia offered.

Doyle flashed her a warning look. Cordelia took a single token sip. She had to get something in her stomach before she drank any alcohol.

As if he read her mind, Slamet took her glass and said, "Please follow me. We have a special house for the *sedhekah*. These other guests are here for the reception."

Cordelia took that in, flattered to be of the elite. *Which is like it should be*, she reminded herself. *And would have been, if Daddy hadn't lost all his money.*

With a snap of Slamet's fingers, another servant appeared. He was carrying a small black scarf.

"Please, Miss Chase, don't be offended. This is traditional," Slamet said.

"Excuse me?"

He opened the scarf and held it up. "*Adat* requires that women may not see the path to the place of the *sedhekah*. Back in Indonesia, you wouldn't even be able to attend."

"You want to blindfold me?" she asked incredulously. She looked at Doyle, who was frowning.

"Only for a few moments. Perhaps as long as two minutes." He smiled. "We're in a public place. Nothing will happen to you here."

She touched her hand to her chest. "Actually, technically, um, since this is your compound, it's not a public place. *Oh.*" She stared at Doyle.

He stared back.

Not a public place.

Angel will need to be invited to get onto the compound, or he won't be able to take one single step onto it.

It was part of his vampire deal: he couldn't so

much as walk into her apartment if she didn't invite him the first time.

She looked past Doyle to see an L.A. police car driving slowly through the crowd. It was leaving.

"But we're being carefully protected," he said, looking in the same direction. "As wealthy people, we're always careful. Always friendly with the authorities, and always very polite in our adopted countries."

He took her hand and brushed his lips against her knuckles, looking up at her with his dark, soulful eyes.

"No harm will come to you. I promise it."

Doyle said, "What about me?"

Slamet chuckled. "No harm to you, either."

Doyle gestured to the scarf. "You've only got one blindfold."

"You're a man," Slamet said.

"Yeah." Doyle sounded as if he wasn't sure. He glanced at Cordy. "I'm not feeling too well. Would you mind very much if we left?"

She hesitated. Then she thought, *What am I doing? It's definitely time to book.*

"Okay, Doyle. I'm so sorry," she murmured to Slamet. "He's had a lot of health problems ever since, um, the war."

"Hey," Doyle protested, then clamped his mouth shut.

"War?" Slamet looked puzzled.

"Yeah, so . . . limo?"

"Of course. Let me have it brought around." Slamet looked dithery. "It might take a few minutes."

"But it was just here," Cordelia said.

"It's crowded on the compound," Slamet explained.

He gestured for a very beefy looking guy to walk over. The guy had on a suit but he didn't look at all like the suit type. He looked more like the muscle-tee-on-the-beach type.

He came over and folded his hands in front of himself.

"Please see to our guests," Slamet told him. Then he inclined his head and walked away.

"I'm not liking this," Cordelia murmured.

"Me, neither," Doyle muttered under his breath. "And I can't exactly fight my way out of here with this many people around."

She closed her eyes and murmured, "I invite you, I invite you, I invite you."

"Tap your heels together three times," Doyle suggested.

"Oh. Okay." She did so.

In an amused tone, he said, "Now repeat after me, 'There's no place like home.' "

"Ha ha. Very funny." She opened her eyes. "Doesn't work, huh?"

"Cordy, if you could just throw out random invitations to vampires on the wind like that, there'd be no point to it."

"And there is now?" she asked.

He nodded. "It's all quite complicated. Believe me, it's complicated." He rolled his eyes. "So's the fact that human beings need to sleep. But nevertheless, it is a fact."

"Okay." She didn't get it. But she supposed it didn't matter. "Let's just get out of here, okay?"

Then she sighed. "Why is it that all the rich men in this town turn out to be evil? When I had money, I wasn't evil."

"It's what you have to do to get rich in this town," Doyle suggested. "Or maybe it's just an unfortunate coincidence that you keep running into the men who believe that."

Slamet found Jusef with Meg. She was slumped in one of the high-backed wicker chairs Slamet's aunt—Jusef's mother—had always preferred. Jusef was seated across from her. He had a cell phone on his lap and he was sipping a glass of champagne.

Slamet hurried up to them. He did another double take as he looked down on the young woman. Her eyes were glazed and her jaw was slack. But other than a few slight—and superficial—differences, she and Cordelia Chase bore an amazing resemblance to each other.

"Slamet," Jusef said. "Good." He tapped his cell phone. "I've got interesting news. When the limo went to pick up Cordelia Chase, she had two men with her."

Slamet frowned. "Two?"

"And all three of them were carrying protective amulets. Against various subspecies of Asian demons."

Slamet's lips parted.

"And she seemed like such a nice girl," Jusef drawled. "This is some kind of setup. They know who we are."

"Two men."

Jusef took another sip of champagne. He looked relaxed, but Slamet saw that his hand was trembling.

If Jusef's frightened, we're in bad trouble, he thought worriedly.

"She only showed up with one," Slamet told him.

"I know. The other one just beat the crap out of two of our best." He drained off the champagne. "But listen to this, Slamet. Someone moved the body of Ernesto Torres. To a very public location."

"Who would do that?" Slamet asked, even more worried.

"Someone who wants us to get caught."

Without warning, Jusef flung his champagne glass to the ground. The delicate crystal shattered into dozens of brittle shards that ricocheted into the air.

"A traitor. We seem to have an awful lot of them in our midst, don't we?"

Slamet ran his hands through his hair. "What are we going to do?"

"Yes?" Jusef asked sharply.

A servant stood in the door. His voice was measured and respectful.

"*Pak*, the guests are waiting for the *sedhekah* to begin."

"What are we going to do?" Slamet asked. "What's the use of anything? With your father dead . . ."

Jusef silenced him with a thundering look. Slamet closed his mouth.

"We'll be there in a minute," Jusef snapped.

"Yes, *pak*," the servant replied. He bowed his head and withdrew.

"Everything's unraveling. It's unraveling," Slamet said. His voice was shrill.

"Calm down," Jusef barked. "Let me think."

Meg was *there* in the room. She was aware.

She couldn't move, but she could see, and hear, and think.

She saw Jusef take the hypodermic needle out of a leather case. She saw him plunge it into a vial and pull it back out. The barrel was filled with something green and viscous.

No, she begged as he positioned the needle against the crown of her head.

He pushed the needle in.

How it penetrated her skull, she did not know. And she had heard once upon a time that the brain felt no pain. It was possible to operate on it without anesthesia, if need be.

But she felt every millimeter of the sharp needle as it was thrust inside her head. Past a sting, it was the most painful sensation she had ever felt. It made her eyes bulge and ache. The inside of her nose throbbed. The back of her head felt as if it had erupted into flame.

He's killing me, she thought wildly.

Summoning her force of will, she tried to do everything she could to stop him. But she could only lie limply in her chair like a string puppet, staring at him.

"Meg?" he asked, moving his face toward hers. "Meg, are you awake?"

How long have you been doing this to me? she thought. *Why have you been doing this to me?*

She said nothing, did nothing. He seemed satisfied that she was unconscious.

He put the needle back in the case and snapped it shut. In the quiet of the sitting room, the sound was so startling that she would have jumped out of the chair if she had been able to move. But she couldn't.

So maybe that's what's saving my life right now.

"When I count to ten, you'll awaken," he said to

her. "Meg, when I count to ten, you will remember none of this."

Yes, I will. I will. I will.

I'll remember everything.

Angel?

I'll remember everything.

Angel?

"One, two, three, four . . ."

Cordy and Doyle were still trying to decide what to do. She had her hand in her purse on her cell phone.

"If I call the police, they might pick up my signal," Cordelia said.

"If they're on the up and up, they'll be pissed off for the embarrassment, but that'll be the extent of it," Doyle observed. "If they're not cool, we want them to know the police are on their way."

"Okay, then." Cordelia flipped open her cell phone. "Oh." She bit her lower lip. "Battery's dead."

Just then, their limo rolled up.

And Jusef Rais was striding quickly toward him.

"I understand there's been an illness," he said. "I'm so sorry."

"Yes. We have to go," Cordelia said firmly. "Now."

Jusef opened the limo door. "May I call you?" he asked.

"Oh, God, I'm surprised you still want to," she blurted, then caught herself. "That'd be nice."

"Do you have a card?" he queried. "Something to write on?"

"Um, no, not on me."

"What's that?" he asked.

Cordelia and Doyle both turned around. Cordelia swallowed. One of Angel's business cards sat on the leather seat.

"Oh, good, I thought I'd lost that," she said.

Doyle moved to the door to retrieve the card, but Jusef got to it first.

"Angel Investigations?" he asked, looking long and hard at it. Probably at the address, Doyle figured. Then her eyes widened as she saw her purse on the soft leather seat.

"Oh, it's this side . . . it's a business a friend of mine runs," she said. "Like he's a guardian angel. For helpless . . . teen runaways," she finished lamely. She glanced at Doyle.

"Yeah," Doyle said. "We give him a hand now and then."

"Or, used to. Actually, we're no longer friends," she continued. "It was all just too . . . grubby, you know? I mean, those kids hardly ever wash." She shrugged. "I've been meaning to toss these cards out, but I keep forgetting."

"You're not in contact with him anymore, this friend?" Jusef asked.

"No way. I haven't talked to him in, oh, months."

"Me, neither." Doyle held his hand out. "We'll just toss that."

"No, you can write your current phone number on it," Jusef told Cordelia.

"Oh." She shrugged. "Got a pen?"

He produced a beautiful Mont Blanc fountain pen. She gave it a second glance, then scribbled down a fake number.

"There." She handed it to him.

"Well, I'm very sorry your evening was cut short," Jusef said earnestly.

"Thanks. Good night," she said.

"Good night," Doyle added.

Jusef picked up her hand and brushed her knuckles with his lips. Doyle took her other hand and urged her into the vehicle.

They got settled.

As the limo glided through the gates, Doyle thought he heard a shriek.

Cordelia gasped. "What was that?" she said to Doyle.

Pressing her face against the tinted glass, she tried to roll down the window. It wouldn't budge.

Doyle turned on the speakerphone that patched them them through to the chauffeur.

"Did you hear that?"

"Yes, *pak*. It was a peacock," the man said.

"Oh." Cordelia looked at Doyle and gave a fakey

little laugh. "It sounded like someone being mur-
dered, for heaven's sake."

"Yes, *ibu*," the chauffeur said. "It did."

They drove through Checkpoint Charlie. Then
something sweet wafted through the spacious leather
interior.

Doyle glanced worriedly at Cordelia.

"Maybe it's car deodorizer," she said hopefully.
"Do you, um, see any of those little Christmas trees
dangling somewhere?"

"Cordy, give me your talisman," Doyle said.

Then his head fell back against the seat.

"Doyle? Doyle?" she asked frantically. "Help!"

She pounded on the window that separated them
from the driver. There was no response.

"No. Help," she murmured.

She tried to see if a little Christmas tree was dangling from the rearview mirror, but the window
between her and the chauffeur was too darkly
tinted.

Everything slid sideways. She began to spin.

I invite you. I invite you, she thought fuzzily,
fighting to stay awake. *Angel, I'm sending out an
S.O.S. RSVP, please.*

Please, please, please.

Her eyes closed.

The limo glided on.

161

CHAPTER EIGHT

Angel got a speeding ticket on the way to the Rais compound.

He stood seething while the cop made a big show out of calling in his driver's license and registration, making it absolutely clear that no one went forty miles over the speed limit on *his* watch, thank you very much.

This kind of thing doesn't happen in the movies, Angel thought as he waited for his impeccable credentials to be declared impeccable. *Okay, maybe to someone like Indiana Jones.*

Not such bad company.

"All right. Everything checks out," announced tonight's poster guy for law and order. "You keep this up, the next funeral you're going to will be yours. Or someone else's," he finished with a flourish.

It was a struggle not to state the obvious, but

Angel managed. He even accepted the ticket and the astronomical fine attached to it with a good grace.

"Don't try to fight it," the cop added, as Angel put the car in gear. "I've got the record in my division for most convictions."

Even through that, Angel kept his calm.

But after he drove away, he was so furious he began to morph into his true face. He felt it, and confirmed it by pressing his fingertips against his fangs and ridged brow. Looking in the rearview mirror was useless, of course.

But realizing he had begun to vamp reminded him that the Rais compound was private property. He wasn't going to be handed any invitations onto it any time soon.

Do they know I'm a vampire? he wondered. *Did the talismans tip them off, or did they already know who I was? And why do they care?*

And who's Latura?

He drove like a crazy man, ready, willing, and able to get another speeding ticket, hoping he could keep his cool if he did. Road rage could easily become an occupational habit in L.A., it seemed like. But lives were at stake, and each second counted.

The lives of those closest to me, he thought. *I've buried so many friends.*

Part of the reason I moved here was so I wouldn't have any.

But it didn't appear that the Powers That Be were going to let him off the hook that easily. Doyle liked to point out that to save people, he had to know people. "Get involved. Mix with 'em."

Otherwise, Doyle asserted, they would mean nothing to him. Humanity would become a faceless blur to him.

And that's bad why?

Because caring about a person made him, Angel, more of a person and less of a demon, he supposed. To demons, humans were targets. Prey.

They were pretty much interchangeable. That took away their uniqueness.

That denied the importance of their souls.

Which brought him back to the remorse thing. As long as he could remember his victims, face by face, name by name, if he knew them—as long as he suffered on behalf of each one, he kept his own soul intact.

No man's an island. He could almost hear Doyle saying words to that effect.

Yeah, and there's lots of fish in the sea.

And that would be something Cordelia would say.

Help me.

Angel, help me.

He nearly slammed on the brakes.

It was the voice again.

And she knew who he was.

Help me, he sent back, in case they had a two-way connection.

Meg looked up at Jusef and tried to hide the terror in her eyes. He cocked his head and said, "Are you all right?"

She was having trouble walking. She felt numb from head to toe.

"I want you to dance tonight," he said. "Can you do that for me?"

Can I put a knife through your eye? she thought, savage with fury. Yet she kept it tamped down.

Just like everything else.

"We'll go down to the club after all this stuff, okay? Let loose."

She nodded. "I'm really tense."

"I can feel it." He eyed her. "Didn't the session help you?"

"I feel pretty good, considering." She touched her head. "My head hurts a little."

He regarded her sadly. She knew he was trying to make her think about the tumor.

I don't have one, she realized. *He made me think I was dying so he could keep doing whatever it is he's doing to me.*

His arm was like iron around her waist. She gave

him a sad smile in return and said, "Do you mind if I lie down? I'd like to rest up for the performance."

"We'll make it your debut," he suggested. "I'll invite some guys to the club and we'll record it, all right?"

"That would be a dream come true."

She couldn't believe it. Maybe it had once been a dream, but no longer.

Then she thought, *Maybe the shots are to make the tumor go away. Maybe I've misunderstood. He didn't want to tell me because he didn't want to scare me. Or give me false hope.*

She looked up at him.

"Jusef?"

His smile was so incredible. It was like the sun. "Yes?"

She searched his face. A wariness crossed over his features. It wouldn't be there if he didn't have something to hide.

Her insides quavered.

I can't say a word, she thought. *If I say anything, he'll know I've lost faith in him.*

"What, Meg?"

"Do you think we'll be famous?"

"I can pretty much guarantee it."

Angel roared toward the compound, trying to formulate a plan.

But as he came in sight of the gates, he still didn't have one.

I don't have enough information, he thought, frustrated. *I don't know what I'm fighting.*

Except a really brutal kind of dying.

He pulled off the road and killed the engine. He watched the gate. If someone came along on foot, he could saunter up, turn on the charm, and maybe fake his way onto the grounds with them.

And there's where the mixing-in part comes in yet again, Angel thought. *My so-nonexistent charm.*

He thought of his Galway days as a wastrel, when he could charm almost any colleen into the hay barn. Even proud beauties like Dorrie.

He wondered what had ever become of her.

Nias, 1930

Alice Kenney said to Father Van Der Putten, "Why Nias? Why not? I've always been drawn to the place."

She pulled her cloche over her forehead. Her feet were baking in her black boots. The sun was ghastly. She was going to freckle. The mosquitoes were biting her; if she didn't die from the heat, surely she would from loss of blood.

"It has great mystical importance to the natives," the Dutch father informed her. He spoke beautiful

English. She wondered if he had requested this posting, or if he'd simply been assigned it willy-nilly.

He continued, "They believe one of their gods lives beneath the village. A sort of hellish demon."

"Good heavens." She touched her chest. A beautiful Celtic cross lay across her white blouse.

"It's superstition, of course," he added.

They smiled at each other in tolerant amusement. Then Alice said, "I suppose one can't expect savages in the middle of nowhere to be very sophisticated. In my own family, it was believed one of my ancestresses was a witch."

"How fascinating." He raised his brows. "I'm very keen on that sort of thing. That's why I asked to be sent here."

Ah. That answers one question.

The other is . . . How observant a priest is he?

The good father was rather handsome. Alice, for all her wishing to devote her fortune to good deeds, was still a youngish woman.

In this day and age, twenty-seven is still young, she thought defensively. But she knew that at home in Galway, they were happy to see her go abroad. She'd failed to land any of the available men, and it was disheartening for a family of beauties to have their sole plain girl teetering on the brink of being an old maid.

So it's been a bit of a blessing, she thought. *I get*

to do all the things they won't permit the pretty ones to do.

"Here's where you'll stay," Father Van Der Putten told her.

She stopped. It was a charming cottage made of wood. It rather resembled a tree house, with chintz curtains and a brick chimney. Though when one would need a fire in this overheated greenhouse of a country, she had no earthly idea.

"I'm sure you'll want to rest before dinner," he continued as he opened the door.

It was quite sweet, if very small. The single room featured a cot, a wooden chair, and a very tiny table. She noted the presence of an oil lamp and several candles.

Over the cot hung a large and somewhat grue-some crucifix. The wounds of Christ were deep and very bloody. She swallowed, a trifle put off, but loathe to mention such a thing to a priest.

"Do you . . . ?" She laughed.

He smiled at her. "Yes?"

"I was about to ask you if you dress for dinner."

"Indeed we do." He gestured to his clerical collar. "I'll have on my finest. And the good sisters as well."

She was abashed.

He said gently, "Please, wear whatever makes you comfortable in this heat. We stand on ritual, but not on ceremony."

She laughed at his joke. "Your English is excellent."

"I wish my Javanese were equal to it," he admitted. "I can't seem to make myself understood to those with whom I wish to communicate most."

"Well, do remember, Father, that they're primitives."

"I try." He sighed. Then he brightened. "At any rate, I know everyone will enjoy dinner tonight, with such a fascinating new dinner companion."

"Hardly fascinating." She blushed.

Their gazes caught, met. He didn't look away. The smile on his face grew slightly mischievous. Very tantalizing.

"Very fascinating," he countered.

Then he left her, shutting the door.

She felt quite self-conscious, disrobing, knowing he was out there somewhere. She remained in her chemise only, taking off her stockings and other heavy underclothes.

She lay on the cot—*clean sheets; good heavens, how do they do the wash out here?*—and tried to think about her purpose for being here. She had heard about Nias from the Sisters of Charity in Galway. The exotic land of Java was also a pagan land, filled with mystery perhaps, but also rampant disease and ignorance. Alice, an educated woman, could do so much good there, helping the nuns and the priest with educating the natives. The little

church of Our Lady of Perpetual Mercy was struggling along, and it could certainly use another civilized white person in the midst of all that . . . *yellow*.

"I'm not sure I'm all that civilized," she murmured to the mosquito netting as she pulled it over
herself. The mosquitoes were buzzing around her
ears, making an astonishing amount of noise. They
were buffeting her earlobes with such rapidity and
force that they sounded like thunder.

No.

Like drums.

Or is that my heart?

She was the star at dinner, and good thing, too,
because she had no idea what she was eating and no
desire to find out. The food was extremely hot, and
bits of it were chewy and leathery. It had to be
some kind of unknown flesh.

Very little settled in her stomach; she talked so
much, trying out her broken Dutch, moved to near
tears by the eagerness of the nuns to hear about
"home," by which they meant anywhere in Europe.
Their longing made her wonder about her own
commitment to stay here for at least six months. No
one would come for her before then.

She was on her own, out here in the jungle.

Her journal helped.

ANGEL

April 20, 1920

I've been here for three weeks, and settled in, I think, to a fairly regular routine. I help the sisters clean the little church every morning, and then we prepare breakfast. Father Van Der Putten, as the only male in our henhouse, seems to enjoy swaggering about. For all they're brides of Christ, I must confess that the sisters don't mind his attentions in the least, commenting as he does on their rosy cheeks and bright eyes of a morning.

But the roses come from sunburning, and they're all leathery and rather old-looking. In comparison, I'm practically a dewy debutante. What an irony, then, that the only man worth having about stands on his vows, at least thus far.

Of a night, I hear the mosquito-drums, as I've come to call them. I actually find myself waiting for them, else I can't sleep. It's uncanny how much their droning sounds like actual drums. I've mentioned the phenomenon a number of times to the others, but no one else makes the same connection. They've wondered aloud if something about the construction of the cottage makes them sound the way they do.

But I think it's part of my fanciful nature.

"Or perhaps it's your witchcraft," Father Van Der Putten said after vespers last evening. "The beast below is calling you."

He chuckled when he said it, but I do believe that he half-believed what he was saying.

Sometime in June, 1920

Ah, you see? It must be June, at least. I can no longer keep track of dates. Only months. Father Van Der Putten tells me that if I stay here longer than a year, after a time I shall begin to lose track of the months. Merciful heaven! What an existence.

I've finally met the natives. It's incredible to realize that they're capable of savagery that would send the typical Irish girl screaming in terror. Though they're pleasant enough to me, Father Van Der Putten tells me that shortly before my arrival, their warriors went on a raiding party. Dressed in their traditional finery—black jackets and plumed heads, like birds of prey—they butchered ten men from another village and brought back their heads.

This they did, he now informs me, because "the god below" told them that he would rise soon, as a vessel was being prepared for him.

He believes the vessel may have been the large circle of skulls they created from the heads of the vanquished. Indeed, sure and as I'm standing here, they showed me that on my first visit, smiling and gesturing to me.

The headman has a son perhaps eight years my

junior, and it seems he expects we shall marry. Or whatever it is they do to establish a bond between each other. The good Father has jested that he'll perform a good Catholic wedding, and the nuns are very jolly about it as well.

I must confess that he is very handsome, and well-formed, but of course it is all so ridiculous.

Angel got out of the car. There was a stand of pepper trees to his right, their fragrance a sort of odd counterpoint to his situation. He had no idea if Doyle and Cordelia were in trouble—he wouldn't let himself think anything worse than that—but here were the trees, wafting of pepper as if all was right with the world. In the grit of the city, evil was at home. But out in nature, which was generally a neutral third party, battles against the forces of darkness felt misplaced.

He moved among the trees, a shadow melting into shadow, listening to the noises of the reception. Moving forward, he spotted an electric fence, strung ankle-height, and stayed on its outer perimeter.

I should've packed weapons, he thought. *Or at least run back for a few before I took off.*

His attackers had been unarmed except for their chop-socky routines.

He kept walking, looking for a chink in the compound's defenses. Then he ran up against the wall of the next-door neighbor's.

Californians were nothing if not known for their devotion to fencing in their property.

There seemed to be no way to crash the party, though.

Then he heard someone whisper, "Are you there?"

He stopped moving. If he breathed, he would have stopped breathing. He did everything he could to make himself undetectable.

"It's me."

The woman in his head.

He turned his head over his shoulder.

She was facing him.

"How'd you get here?" he said without preamble.

She said nothing. Her face was white. Her eyes stared straight ahead.

"Oh, no." She clutched her head and began to cry. "It's forgotten. It's all forgotten!"

Then she fainted.

Nias, 1997

The night air was clogged with the overwhelming odor of burning human flesh; and beneath that, the stench of flaming tires and oil and eucalyptus trees. Incredibly, Meg could still catch the faint traces of her own perfume beneath the coppery odor of blood as it ran down her face.

They had arrived at dusk, her favorite time of day. The stillness reminded her of Heaven; sandalwood scented the air and the monkeys rustled in the lush forest overgrowth. She and her tiny charges, at five and six the youngest boarders at Our Lady of Perpetual Mercy, had been on their way to mass.

From the jungle, masked men rushed them, shrieking and shooting their weapons. The girls had screamed and run off in all directions, only to be caught by the soldiers and dragged back into a huddle.

Then they came at Meg like *orang pendek*, half-man, half-beast, in a blur of rifles and masks and fists. The little girls stood all in a row, watching, as the invaders beat her, and worse. More than once, she forced herself not to give in to the luxury of losing consciousness. She had to do everything she could to protect her girls.

Hours went by. They would let her rest in her own blood on the ground, then revive her and start her torture all over. They asked nothing of her. The sky had lowered and all traces of daylight were gone. The night was alive with fires. The dormitories were on fire; the church itself, an old Dutch colonial mission, was a smoldering ruin.

Finally one of them grabbed her hair and yanked

back her head. He held a machete to her throat that was caked with dried blood.

"Where is the *pustaha lakak?*" he asked in a garbled voice.

She was stunned. She actually laughed in despair. The man smacked her hard against the cheek with the flat side of the blade.

"Tell us, or one by one we'll kill the girls."

She fought to get her hysteria under control. But in a hideous way, this was all unbearably funny. It was like hearing one of those ghoulish stories about an arsonist who died lighting a birthday cake. Only this was happening to her and her little girls; this was really happening to her.

"It doesn't exist," she managed, and another round of uncontrollable laughter threatened to bubble out of her. She opened her swollen eyes, but everything was bloody and clouded. "It's a myth."

Local legend had it that an Irishwoman had come here years before and made love to a buried god. It had driven her mad. She spent the rest of her life walled up inside the church, scribbling insanely in a *pustaha lakek,* a magick book.

In Indonesia, such books were written on bark, usually in Sanskrit. No matter to the legend that this woman wouldn't know anything about Sanskrit, and certainly wouldn't have gotten hold of a blank book made of bark.

Be that as it may, this *pustaha lakek* was reputed to describe the nature and being of Latura, ancient God of the Dead. The original teachings of Latura had been handed down by a Badui village woman who had come to live among the Nias. Her descendants, it was claimed, learned all the words of the unholy teachings by rote.

Then the Irishwoman had arrived and written everything down. Then Latura possessed a sacred Book, as did many gods of antiquity whose worship had been refined and passed down through the spoken word for generation upon generation.

To bring Latura forth, one must precisely chant the proper spells and incantations, and perform the correct sacrifices. It was a given that Latura required many sacrifices. After all, his earliest worshipers had been cannibals and headhunters.

But in attempting to call Latura forth, the mad Irishwoman's heart had caught fire. She had burned to death, from the inside out. The Book, however, had not burned. If one dug up her skeleton, they would find charred arms clasping the bark book to her rib cage.

Meg's spiritual adviser, Father Hendrik, had confided to Meg that they had indeed found a book buried with a charred fifty-year-old female skeleton, in 1983. But it was a Christian Bible the bony arms had held, not a damned book of the Devil.

Meg realized now that the story must have gotten out—most likely, the servants had talked—and now someone very evil had come for the Book of Latura.

Father Hendrik, always her rock in times of trouble—he had married her parents and baptized her and all her brothers and sisters—lay in the infirmary on this night of terror. He had been ailing for the last six days from some mysterious malady. The local *dukun* insisted that he had been cursed by an enemy. Meg was shocked to realize that despite her upbringing in the church, she was convinced that the leader of these men was the one who had made Father Hendrick sick. With evil magick, and through traditional, forbidden rituals.

"Where is the Book?" they demanded, over and over, hitting her savagely each time they repeated the question. They threatened to fling her into the burning church, along with the children.

Then they dragged Father Hendrik from his sick bed. She was shocked to see him in his hospital gown, his bright red hair nearly gone, his face wasted and gray. He was little more than a skeleton himself, when a week ago, he had been vigorous despite his years.

They saw each other. His look of shock must have been as great as her own.

"Mary Margaret," he groaned, using her Christian

name. He raised a shaking hand and tried to make the sign of the cross. One of the men socked him on the shoulder. Father Hendrik cried out and stumbled forward.

"Tell us, or he dies," the leader said.

"Meg, don't," Father Hendrik blurted.

The leader threw back his head and laughed.

"So, do you still claim that there's no Book?" he demanded, cuffing Meg.

She stared in bewilderment at the priest. Of course there was no Book. Or had he lied to her?

"He knows where it is," the leader announced.

They turned all their cruelty on the priest. Meg blacked out as his screams reached fever pitch.

When she came to, they had bound him hand and foot. He was lying beside her. His hospital gown was soaked with his blood. His face barely looked human, it was so bruised.

He looked straight at her and said softly, "There's a *kris*." Quickly, he glanced back at his torturers, who had not heard. "I don't know where it is."

Then they held her head and made her watch as they pushed him into the smoldering church.

In the absence of a blaze, it took him a long time to die.

The dozen Dutch and Dutch-Indonesian nuns were next.

The leader sent men to her village, taunting her,

describing in detail what they would do there. Hours later they returned with her father's head.

After what they had done to Meg, she prayed that her mother, a religious woman, was dead as well.

Then it was almost dawn. The leader said, "I applaud your loyalty to whatever sorcerer you serve. We were told of your strong blood ties to the Book. But the time has come to tell us the rest. Or with first light, our master will eat your soul. Believe me, death is far preferable."

She was confused. *Blood ties?* "What rest? What is the rest?" she begged.

What had happened next, Meg had always assumed was a delusion brought on by terror and pain.

Silhouetted by firelight, the leader clapped his hands. As one, he and all his men tore off their masks

As one, she and the little girls screamed. Meg vomited blood.

She had never seen anything more revolting in her life. Their faces were a sickly, diseased green, their foreheads and cheeks slashed with deep, red welts that pulsed and oozed. Their eyes were elongated and yellow, the pupils narrow and lozenge-shaped. They darted and hissed at her like poisonous snakes.

"We are *jin*," the leader had told her. "Demons. We rise from the pits to rip away the souls of the dead as they fly to heaven. You can rest assured our master has fed well today."

She sobbed. "I don't know, I don't know."

"Hold her," the leader said.

His face grew. It stretched from forehead to chin by at least a meter; as she watched in horror, rows and rows of teeth grew in crosshatches over his face. His eyes receded and teeth grew in the sockets.

"There's much darkness in you," he hissed, his voice raspy and soft. "There's much to eat."

The teeth extended forward, separating from what had once been his face except for thin filaments of pulsating, blue protrusions.

"The Book—where is it?"

"I don't know, please, please!"

The teeth bulleted toward her. The first one to reach her pierced her cheek, and she shrieked wildly and closed her eyes.

Then nothing touched her. She opened her eyes.

The demon was gone, and his followers with him.

All that remained was a shower of iridescent blue sparks.

In the distance someone shouted.

Meg crumpled to the ground.

CHAPTER NINE

Cordelia was dreaming about shopping. All the stores carried her size only, and all the shoes were not only fashionable and comfortable, but *good for her feet*. In fact, if you clicked them together three times—

"There's no place like home," she mumbled.

"Miss, miss, wake up," said a man with an accent.

Then she was being half-carried, half-dragged into warm, fresh air. Her dress caught on a sticker bush, but she was pushed forward. Her pantyhose ripped.

She began coughing. Her eyes rolled back in her head when she tried to open her lids. Someone was pounding her on the back.

She yowled, "Ow!" and pulled herself out of someone's arms.

It was a frail man the color of walnut dressed as a Catholic priest. Beside him, watching very intently, was the little girl who had left the note in her purse.

Cordelia said fuzzily, "Celia?"

The girl broke into a smile. "That's *me, ibu*."

"Cordelia," Cordelia said. She rubbed her fore-head. She had a terrible headache. "Where's Doyle? What's going on?"

"I'm Father Wahid," the priest told her gently. "Your friend is going to be all right." He gestured to the right of the limo, which was canted at an odd angle on a deserted road. They were on a hill, over-looking the lights of the city.

"Hey," Doyle said, hanging his head out the limo's door and giving her a slack smile. "How about this?"

"What is the 'this' that this *is*?" Cordelia de-manded. "What did you guys do, rob the limo?"

"No, no," Father Wahid said quickly. "We saved your lives. They were going to kill you."

"Slice you up," the little girl said, in a bizarrely cheerful tone of voice.

"Celia," the priest reproved.

Cordelia tried to get to her feet. "Where's the driver?" She winced. "My head is killing me."

"We knocked him out," the good Father informed her. "Which is a hell of a lot better than what he was planning to do to you."

"Father, don't say *hell*," Celia said, imitating his stern voice.

"Forgive me, my child." He smiled kindly at Doyle as Doyle walked unsteadily toward them. "How are you feeling?"

"Like I do when I have a vision," he told Cordelia. To the priest, he replied, "Like someone set an explosion off inside my head."

Doyle regarded the priest. "Who are you, anyway, and how did you find us?"

"And what do you want?" Cordelia added.

"First and foremost, to save your lives," Father Wahid said. He indicated his clerical collar with a bit of self-mockery. "I am a servant of God," he observed.

"And secondly, since we both battle a common enemy, I wish to join forces."

"That enemy being . . . ?" Cordelia asked suspiciously.

The priest shrugged as if the answer were obvious. "The Devil."

She traded looks with Doyle, then moved her shoulders. "Works for me."

"How do you know we're battling the Devil?" Doyle asked. "For all you know, we were on the Devil's side, and we had too much to drink at the wake for Bang Rais. Passed out in the back of our limousine, as it were."

Father Wahid cocked his head. "You don't know about the *jin,* do you?"

"Father, I'm Irish," Doyle retorted. "I know about every form of alcohol ever fermented or brewed."

"That's such a stereotype," Cordelia said. "Have you ever had Kristal champagne?"

Doyle thought a moment.

"Can't say that, no."

She was only slightly dashed.

"Okay," she said to the priest. "So, gin."

"*Jin*. Demons. Agents of the supernatural. There are good ones, and bad."

"That's hard to believe." Cordelia rolled her eyes. "About the good ones, I mean. I've never met a demon I could stand. Except for my boss. And he's a special case."

Father Wahid frowned and looked at Doyle. "But what about . . . ? Never mind."

"Angel's a special case," Cordelia repeated. "But I wouldn't go so far as to say he's a good demon. A good guy, maybe." She wrinkled her nose. "Not that good a boss, because the pay sucks. But on the other hand, he doesn't want to charge people for helping them, and—"

Father Wahid cleared his throat. "I have employed *jin* to help me in my battle."

"Angels," Celia cut in.

The priest tousled her hair. "Angels. What else can they be?"

"Demons?" Doyle ventured.

"We just went through that," Cordelia said impatiently. "There's no such thing as a good demon."

"Right. I forgot," he drawled.

"My *jin* detected the talismans you had with you. As did the Raises. They flew to me and let me know. And Celia and I ventured out of hiding to save you."

"So, they're kind of like carrier pigeons," Cordelia said.

"More like the probes in *Star Wars*," Father Wahid replied.

"Okay. All that's fine. If you believe it," Cordelia muttered under her breath. "But what's up with fighting the Raises? I mean, Devil, Raises. They're not exactly, um, you know, the exact same."

Father Wahid's features hardened. His blue eyes became steely. He said, "The Raises have massacred hundreds, if not thousands, of the weak and the helpless. They've brought legions of illegal immigrants into this city, only to work them practically to death, and then to sacrifice them to their god."

"So you're a political activist." Doyle massaged his temples. "Which is good. We need people like that. But these guys are maybe doing something really weird, like burning people from the inside out."

"They worship Latura, the God of the Dead," the priest said. "Latura demands sacrifices by the hundreds. With the proper rites and incantations, he can be brought forth to walk upon the Earth.

"If that ever happens, everything he so much as looks upon, and everything—and everyone—he touches, will burst into flame and die. Then he will devour their soul. Their place in the universe will cease to exist."

"You mean, they'll die," Cordelia said.

"The place that was meant for them alone will go empty. The balance of this dimension—and all others which hinge upon it—will be permanently destroyed."

"And, um, it will tip?" Cordelia prompted.

Father Wahid sighed heavily. "Reality will die. Chaos will reign. Forever."

"Not a good thing." Cordelia shook her head.

"Not a good thing," the priest agreed.

"What's stopping them?" Doyle asked.

"They don't have all the knowledge they need to achieve their goal." The priest gestured with his hands. "All the writings pertaining to Latura are kept in a single book. It's the only one of its kind. If they find that book, the world is doomed."

"Do you know where it is?" Doyle asked.

Slowly the priest nodded.

"You've got it," Cordelia said.

He nodded again.

"And I need your help to keep it," he said. "The stars are aligning tomorrow night. It will be the most favorable aspect for the triumph of this evil for the next six hundred and sixty-six years. I don't know if the Raises realize that.

"But Latura does."

Cordelia scowled. "That does it. I'm asking for a raise. And aspirin. Father, do you have any aspirin? Or Tylenol?"

"How can we help you?" Doyle asked.

"If the Raises don't know I've got the Book, they soon will. They've been searching for me for a long time. I think one of their *jin* spotted me coming out of my hiding place just now. If that's true, they will array all their demons and dark forces against me.

"They're formidable enemies, believe me."

"Can we just take your word for it?" Cordelia asked. Before anyone could answer, she added, "And am I the only one who's worried about Angel?"

Doyle looked at her. Slowly he shook his head.

"You're not," he told her.

"You can't be serious," Meg said to Angel as he crouched over her by the wall. "They're on full alert all over the compound. If they find you, they'll kill you."

Angel was touched by her concern. "I'm hard to kill," he assured her.

"You don't know the Raises. You don't know what they're capable of."

189

He gave her a hard look. "And do you? Have you just stood by?"

She shook her head. "I didn't know. I'm still not sure."

"Meg," he said sadly. "People have been dying all over the city, in a very horrible way."

"We can't be sure that Jusef's involved. We don't have any proof," she said shrilly.

"Look at me." Angel's voice was kind. Soft. "Meg, look. Somehow, our minds are linked. We're sharing our thoughts."

She hung her head.

"He saved me," she murmured.

Nias, 1998

In the jungle Meg lay on the ground. The rains washed over her. The sun baked her.

Near death, she became delirious. She imagined that an Irishwoman with red hair rose out of her own body and began untying her.

The woman said to Meg, "Remember me always. I am Doreen Kenney. You are of my blood. You are not of these people. You are my decendant. I was left for dead, but I survived. Space and time have lost their hold on us, my girl. Remember that. And live."

✿   ✿   ✿

Weeks later, in the hospital, Meg was told that she had somehow freed herself and wandered alone through the jungle for two weeks.

Her little boarders were never seen again.

Her family had been butchered, presumably by the same men who had left her for dead.

Mary Margaret Taruma—Mary Margaret Kenney —whoever she might be, lost her hold on her world as her identity slid away. She made three attempts to end her life, and she was committed to a mental institution. She drifted there, trying to explain to the doctors that unless she knew, really knew, who she was, she saw no reason to live out a life that might belong to someone else.

They labeled her delusional.

"There is absolutely no point to simply being," she insisted. "If I have no past, I have no future."

They gave her drugs.

They gave her shock therapy.

She began to forget everything that had happened in the jungle. Or more precisely, to lock it away. To bury it so deeply that no one, not even she herself, could access those memories.

But they were not forgotten.

Then one day, inexplicably, she was set free. They came for her, gave her a pair of jeans, some tennis shoes, and a T-shirt—no bra—and led her to the gates of the institution. They opened them and looked at her expectantly.

So she walked through them, momentarily exhilarated by her freedom.

But she agreed soon enough with the old Janis Joplin song: Freedom was just another word for nothing left to lose. She drifted into drugs, and into terrible ways to pay for them.

A year dragged past. Then Jusef Rais had come along. He had found her in a bar, where she was dancing—oh, not the kind of dancing she had learned as a child; not the ancient, proud gestures of the *barong*. No, this was the sad bump-and-grind of lost women, watched with disinterest by defeated men.

That night a stir went through the crowd when Jusef walked in. He was beautifully dressed, in every way the perfect image of an upper-upper-class Indonesian; a man who had made it. In the hot, smoky room, redolent of body odor and cheap cigarettes, he was refined and elegant.

Silently he sat, watching her. Her face burned with shame. He spoke to the manager, who gestured to her after she finished the third of her three required dances and picked up her clothes.

He said, "Mr. Rais wants to see you alone."

She steeled herself. When he had looked at her, he had seen someone he could buy. Why had she allowed herself to stay alive?

Mustering the last ounce of her dignity, she refused to let him ogle her in her dancing costume and put on her street clothes—a faded, modest dress—and wiped off her heavy makeup.

When she entered the room in the back—the one reserved for "private parties"—he stood and applauded softly.

"I knew I was right," he said.

He bought her a glass of wine. She drank it in two gulps. Emboldened by the alcohol, she asked him, "How much are you paying my bosses for me?"

He smiled. His teeth were perfectly white. He said, "I'd like to offer you a job in a band. A real job. A real band. I own a club in California.

"If you'll come with me, I'll make you live forever."

She didn't believe a word of it.

Meg looked at Angel and said, "The apparition said that I'm of the blood. I'm not sure what that means, but I think Jusef knows. I am connected to all this somehow."

He was walking her back through the stand of pepper trees. He said, "Believing that, can you really tell me not to go in there and save my friends?"

She looked frightened. "But you know me. You're the only person in the world who knows me."

"I don't," he said honestly. *Because if I did, you would know me. You would know what I am.*

And you don't.

"I was bitten by some kind of demon, and you've been injected with some kind of serum that must produce similar side effects. I think it's only coincidence that we linked."

"Karma," she said, then smiled wanly. "What would Father Hendrik say? I'm a Catholic. We don't believe in karma."

"Maybe you should," he murmured. Her story had been incredible. If what she had told him was correct, there was a chance that she was the descendant of Dorrie Kenney—or whatever Doreen had become.

My destroyer, he thought.

Is she back again to finish the job?

"You've got to help me," he said firmly.

"But I don't understand. Why do I have to invite you into the compound? You can just walk in."

Angel looked down at her. "Trust me," he said, "and do it. You can walk about freely. No one will question your comings and goings. Just go inside and invite me in."

"You're a sorcerer," she guessed. "My apartment building was owned by a magician, you know. But I think he was just a stage magician. Not a real one."

He wondered if she was chattering because she

was afraid. She had good reason to be. She was taking risks for a stranger.

"Come on." She walked beside him toward the sentry box. After a few steps it was as if someone had thrown on a switch. She smiled calmly and took his hand, swinging it gently as she smiled flirtatiously at the security guard.

"Music critic," she told him. *"Rolling Stone."*

The sentry waved them through.

Just as Angel passed him, the man said, "Wait, *pak*."

Meg caught her breath. Angel raised his brows in brisk politeness and said, "Yes?"

"I disagree with you on Powerman 5000," he said earnestly.

"I didn't write that one."

"Oh." The man moved his shoulders. "I'm glad. Maybe otherwise, I would have to shoot you." He laughed.

Angel smiled. "I'll pass it along."

Meg tripped ahead. Then she turned to Angel with her hands outstretched and said, "Come on in."

He walked onto the compound.

The party or wake or reception was in full swing. The milling crowds were thick; Angel looked for Cordelia and Doyle but realized very quickly it was going to be nearly impossible to spot them.

"Look. There's Jusef," she murmured, turning her back so that the man wouldn't see her.

Angel took note. He also watched two other men join Jusef Rais. They looked left, right, and walked into a small building beside a pond stocked with frogs and carp.

"What's that?" he asked her, once the coast was clear.

She shook her head. "I've never been in there."

Angel decided to take a look.

He said to her, "Wait by the guard kiosk, all right? You need to get out of here."

She looked uncertain. He touched her arm. "Meg, Jusef's been abusing you. He's been poisoning you."

"Or giving me experimental drugs."

"He's using you for something. Trust me."

She took a breath, nodded.

"By the security guard," she echoed.

Angel nodded and started to walk away.

"Be careful," she called softly.

Why start now? he thought.

He moved into the crowd, allowing himself to slowly make his way toward the building. Its dark-blue-tiled roof was square and high, dipping and curving at the ends. The exterior walls were white plaster.

Wooden walkways extended over the carp pond and ended at the front door. As Angel glided along it, a man rushed by, carrying what looked to be a wadded-up black robe in his arms.

Uh-oh, costumes, Angel thought. *Didn't bring one. Not going near the store.*

"Hey," he said to the other man.

The man turned. He looked startled.

"I'm sorry," he said in heavily accented English. "This is a private function."

"I know," Angel replied. He gestured for the man to come closer. "It's just, the thing is . . ." He spoke very quietly.

"I'm sorry, I can't hear you." The man approached. "What?"

"I'm mumbling," Angel mumbled.

"Please speak up," the man said, coming right up to Angel.

Angel put his hand on the man's shoulder. "This is my first meeting. I forgot my robe."

The man frowned. "It is not." He opened his mouth as if he were going to shout.

Angel steadied him with one hand clutching his shoulder, then rammed the fingers of the other hand directly into his solar plexus. The man contracted but Angel held him upright, half-dragging him to the side of the small building.

There, behind some bushes, he let the man slip to the ground. He scooped up the robe and threw it on over his head.

Hood, he noted approvingly. *Hope there's not a password.*

He sent out his thoughts. *Meg?*

He waited.

Meg?

There was no answer. Worse, he no longer felt connected.

He spared a moment of concern for her. Then he hurried around to the door in the center of the front of the building. He pushed it open.

Stairs led downward. If he'd been moving any faster, he would have fallen down them.

He took them easily, as if he had every right to be there.

At the bottom were two doors, one on his right, and one on his left.

How much you want to bet if I open the wrong one, I die?

Just then, a man came out of the one on the right. He was drying his hands. He looked up and gave Angel a brief nod as Angel ducked his head and passed him, grabbing the door before it could close.

He went in.

It was the men's room.

A robed man at the urinal glanced his way, then went back to business.

When in Rome, Angel thought. Casually he crossed the room and went into a stall.

✣   ✣   ✣

Father Wahid laid the unconscious limo driver behind some bushes and said, "If I weren't a priest, I would kill this man."

"It would be a good idea," Cordelia said, making a face. "But so would Ferragamos for less than fifty dollars, and you know that's not gonna happen."

"I was going to go with nuclear fusion, myself," Doyle ventured. At her look, he added, "But shoes are good."

She appeared mollified.

Doyle walked to the limo. The passenger door hung open. He said, "I'll drive."

"You can drive a limousine?" Cordelia asked. "I'm impressed."

"Sure." *Not that I ever have.*

Everyone got in, Celia hovering close to the priest. He put his arm around her and said, "We need to go somewhere safe."

"I vote we go to Angel's," Cordelia suggested. "Not that it's necessarily all that safe, but that if he can, Angel will either show there or call. Plus, there's tons of weapons."

Father Wahid said, "It would be wonderful if he had the *kris.*"

Doyle started the engine. *Gear ratios,* he thought, eyeing the stick shift. *What are they and more important, why does it matter?*

"What's a *kris?*" Cordelia asked.

"In ancient times, they were sacred swords. They could 'cut' words. In Indonesia, we believe in *mandi*. Thoughts, when spoken, take form and become real. Solid. Words. Strung together, they wield great power. They can become spells."

Celia raised her hand as if she were in school. "And prayers."

"Yes, my child," the priest said approvingly.

"Kind of like in comic books?" Cordelia asked. "Those little balloons with the words in them?"

The priest smiled. "Yes, I guess. At any rate, there is a *kris*—just one—that can cut the power of the Book of Latura. If I had it, I could destroy the Book."

"Well, Angel has a lot of weapons," she said. "So there's yet another reason to go to his place. Okay?"

Doyle took a breath and put his foot on the gas. The car shot backward.

"Whoops. Reverse," he muttered. "I knew that."

Seated beside Cordelia, Father Wahid crossed himself and murmured a prayer.

"That goes double for me," Cordelia said.

Angel couldn't help but stare at the epic but grisly architecture of the underground temple. The rib cage that converged overhead; the hundreds, if not thousands, of human skulls lining the walls. The hideous murals—the darkest of nightmares, endowed with form.

I wonder how much this place cost, he thought. *In dollars, if not in lives.*

He looked at the demonic statue reclining around the metal altar—talons, spines, tentacles, fangs—all of it stained with blood.

So that's the big noise, as Spike, my old vampire nemesis and idiot "grandson"—so to speak—would say.

The other men in their long, black robes were standing around a fire in the lowered center of an ornate brass table that resembled the altar. Angel was cautious about getting too close. He didn't look at all like the man whose robe he'd filched.

One of his fellow minions held up a small gong and touched a padded hammer to it. The sound was melancholy.

"In the name of Latura," he intoned.

"Latura," the others chorused.

"Bang Rais is dead. He will not rise." He waited, then smiled. "His son, Jusef, will never die."

"Let it be thus," the group said.

"We have given Latura many sacrifices. We have done all he has asked. Let us continue to do his bidding."

"Latura."

"I have located the Book."

Everyone turned toward the altar, including Angel.

A tall man stood on the burnished metal surface. As he opened his arms, flames rose from the base and flickered a safe distance below him.

He threw back his hood. For a moment, Angel thought he was his adversary from the apartment fire. But while this man resembled the other very closely, he was clearly much younger.

"I, Jusef Rais, have found the Book," he repeated. "And now I will send *jin* to retrieve it."

The others began to cheer and raise their fists. Angel copied them.

Imitation. It's not just the sincerest form of flattery, it's a survival technique.

As the others cheered, large, green, flying monsters flapped from behind the altar. Their faces were snub-nosed, their mouths jutting masses of pointed teeth. With reptilian eyes, they scanned the group. Black, pointed tongues slavered as drool dripped from their mouths.

"They're starving," Jusef explained. "When they bring me the Book, they will feed."

"Latura!" the man beside Angel yelled. The others took up the chant. It went on for at least five minutes.

Which in reality is a very long time.

"Once the Book is in my possession, I will sacrifice thousands for Latura's sake."

"Latura!"

"I will speak the words that will lead our Dread Lord from his eternal hell of darkness."

"Latura!"

"I will give him the vessel in which he shall be reborn."

"Latura!"

"Behold! The vessel!" The man reached down behind himself and grabbed hold of something. He squatted as he leaned over and picked it up.

"Latura!"

He turned back around, rising gracefully as he did so.

"Latura!"

A woman, bound and gagged, lay limp in his arms. Her eyes were blank and dead.

"Latura!"

It was Meg.

CHAPTER TEN

Doyle was just beginning to get the hang of driving the limo when he realized they were getting close to Angel's building.

He didn't think it would be a very good idea for such an ostentatious car to appear outside their building, especially with that Lockley girl breathing down their necks, so he parked on a side street a few blocks away. When he explained his reason to the others, Cordelia murmured, "Well, there *is* a God," and Father Wahid actually chuckled.

They kept to the shadows, for the most part able to skirt around the denizens of the night. One panhandler was especially aggressive, making such a scene that Doyle finally capitulated and gave him what he hoped was a one-dollar bill. It was too dark to tell.

"Thanks, man," the panhandler said. He stepped under a streetlight. He was wearing the most raggedy jeans Doyle had ever seen. Also, a ripped T-shirt featuring a large, very fierce-looking Komodo dragon. Beneath the drawing were the words, CLUB KOMODO.

"Wait," Doyle said, but Cordelia swept up beside him and said, "We'd better hustle, Doyle."

He turned around to find them all looking at him. *I'm in command?*

"I'd better go in first," he said. "Take a look around."

"Good idea," Cordelia told him. Then she put a gentle hand on his shoulder and said, "Be careful."

"Good idea," he replied, mocking her ever so slightly.

They exchanged a smile.

He crossed through the car park and went into the building.

About halfway down the hall, he heard the pitter-patter of feet that sounded like they weighed fifty or sixty pounds each, stomping across the office floor. The ceiling above him shook with each step.

He thought about what to do. It sounded immense. It probably had teeth the size of file cabinet drawers. Any weapon that might stop it was probably downstairs, but he wasn't sure Angel had anything immediately available that would put a dent in it.

While he was debating what to do, the office door into the hall burst open. The creature bounded into the hall, turned, and faced him.

It was a kind of half-iguana, half-mammalian creature. Its mouth cracked open, as huge and silly-looking as a circus clown's, its glowing red eyes reptilian, cold, and scary in the extreme. Its feet were webbed and ended in thick, spiky nails that were split down the middle, almost like hooves.

It was covered with matted hair, sprouted from the crackled skin made of a smooth, hard, stonelike substance.

It was a giant Chia Pet gone terribly wrong.

It stared at Doyle. Then it turned and went back into the office.

Great. Now what?

Then he heard the scraping of the elevator. Then there was a tremendous crash.

He darted into the office.

The creature had somehow wedged its front half into the elevator. Its weight had broken the cable, and the entire thing had fallen to the basement level.

Footfalls pounded outside the open door. Cordelia was the first across the threshold, followed by the priest and the little girl.

"Yow!" Cordelia said, when she saw what had happened.

"It's a *jin*," the priest said. "A form of demon."

"Wonderful. I hope it's got good insurance coverage," Doyle said.

"No. It *is* wonderful," Father Wahid said excitedly. "Rather, it might be wonderful. It was sent here for a reason. Someone must believe your friend has something they want."

He smiled. "My money's on Jusef Rais. And the *kris*."

"But I don't get it," Cordelia said. "How can you be so sure?"

"Because of the nature of *jin*," he said. "They're like . . ." He thought a moment. "Like those pigs in France who dig for truffles. Or hunting hounds. They seek out the essence. They find the scent."

"Then how come they haven't found your Book?" she persisted.

"I've kept it hidden through supernatural means," he said. "But my wards are weakening."

"That used to happen to Willow, back in Sunnydale," Cordelia said, nodding. "It was like her magick got tired." She looked at Doyle. "Willow Rosenberg. I'm sure Angel and I have talked about her."

Doyle nodded. "The witch."

"I believe 'Wicca' is more politically correct," Cordelia informed him.

"Well, whatever she is, we could use her to get downstairs," Doyle said. "That thing's stuck, and it's not happy about it."

Somberly they watched the creature thrash and struggle in the ruined elevator cage.

"Someone has to get down to Angel's apartment," Cordy said. " 'Cuz that's where all the best weapons live."

Heads turned toward Doyle.

He groaned.

"You know, when I got this assignment, I was assured I was to be a messenger only. There was nothing about battling monsters in elevators."

"Here." Cordelia handed him a baseball bat.

He gripped his hands around it and advanced on the creature. It glared at him and roared like the trapped, injured, enraged monster it was.

"If I survive, I'm writing a letter of complaint to the Powers That Be," Doyle announced.

Angel reached out with his mind to Meg, but she wasn't picking up on him.

Maybe her fear is so overwhelming that she can't be reached.

The robed group of followers was disbanding. There was nothing to be done except to leave with the others.

For the moment.

He looked up at her.

I'll be back.

There was no indication that she heard him.

As casually as he could, he sauntered out of the cavern and took the stairs. No one challenged him.

The others were in high spirits, chatting about sacrifices and demons as if they were discussing last night's football game.

He went outside, only to see Jusef emerge from a different set of stairs. Meg was with him. His suit jacket was thrown over her shoulders, which led Angel to believe that beneath it, her hands were still bound. She walked like a zombie.

They disappeared around a corner.

Angel was about to follow when his cell phone went off. He jumped, then grabbed it on the first ring.

"Oh, thank God!" Cordelia cried. "You're alive! Well, technically. Angel, you've got to get over here. You have some kind of sword we need and there's a monster in the elevator."

Despite the seriousness of the situation, he asked, "Did you call a plumber?"

"Ha ha. Very funny. Really. We need you. I shouldn't talk about it on a cell phone, especially if you ever consider running for public office, because someone might listen in. So come home, okay?"

Meg, I'm sorry, he thought.

"All right. I'll get there as fast as I can."

He hung up and put the phone in the pocket of his pants. Uneasily he pulled the robe off over his head and walked back around to where he had left the guy he'd knocked out. He dropped the robe in a heap beside him and walked across the bridge that spanned the carp pond.

No one gave him a second look as he walked toward the gates.

But as he started to climb into his convertible, a large, winged creature swooped down from about fifty yards above him. It was a demon serpent such as he had fought in the blazing apartment, only much, much bigger.

The demon grabbed Angel around the waist with massive, knife-sharp teeth. Angel began to bleed as the creature lifted him off the ground.

Within seconds, they were hundreds of feet above the ground. A fall wouldn't kill him unless he got impaled through his unbeating heart, but the serpent that carried him along had a major death grip on him. It didn't appear to be ready to let go of him any time in the near future. It kept flapping its wings, sailing along on a sea of troubles.

It also didn't look like it was looking for a landing strip anytime soon.

So, flight.

Next time I'm taking the bus, Angel thought as the serpent's talons found new places in his body to slice into.

The moon was huge and yellow, filtering his blood-coated hands a muddy gray. The creature kept flying.

Angel began to fade and doze. Suddenly the serpent stretched open its jaws and hissed, startling the vampire awake. Flame gouted from it mouth, and it wasn't until they went up like torches that Angel realized he and his traveling companion had approached a formation of birds. Those that had been spared cawed frantically, dive-bombing toward the ground.

The serpent didn't follow its flame-broiled targets. It continued on its forward path, not deviating one inch left or right.

What if we reach the mountains? Angel wondered. *Is this thing on some kind of autopilot?*

After a time, he realized he'd dozed off again. He raised his head slowly. It felt like it weighed as much as a car.

Whoa. They'd covered a lot of distance. The shining, mirrored skyscrapers of the City of Los Angeles were getting ready to meet and greet them, possibly to eat them.

"Pull up," Angel grunted. "Pull up!" He pulled at the talons, struggling to extricate himself.

Then the creatures hissed. It opened its mouth and shot flame.

Now what? he thought.

Then he realized what: The serpent was challenging its own reflection in the glass exterior of the hotel formerly known as the Bonaventure.

Its wings flapping violently, it picked up speed and opened its mouth again. It was vomiting flame; huge fireballs rocketed through the night sky and crashed into the exterior of the hotel. Frenzied by the battle, it gripped Angel even more tightly.

People began shrieking. Angel pounded on the talons, clamping his teeth in frustration as the creature held him fast.

He tried to assess his best strategy for impact; all he could think of to do was to tuck his head in and bring up his legs. The effort was almost too much for him.

Buffy, he thought, *don't forget me.*

The serpent charged the wall. The hotel was blazing. The flames made a rushing noise like an immense waterfall.

The world roared in a fire storm; explosions buffeted Angel and nearly ripped his hair from his scalp.

Then he was falling. Through smoke and unbelievable heat and screaming, falling like a boulder.

This is gonna hurt, he thought, trying to stay limp. Your chances were better than if you tensed. *Unless this is* Die Hard V *and I land on an awning, or in the pool—*

He did neither.

Am I hurt?

As he plummeted into unconsciousness, Angel had no idea.

Doyle took a deep breath.

"I would cry, 'For Queen and country,' but y'know, we formed our own government a few months ago," he said.

"I've been meaning to ask you," Cordelia piped up. "Do you have a green card? Because if you're in this country illegally, Angel could face serious jail time. Plus a fine, you know?"

Doyle looked at her with astonishment. "I was sent here by the Powers That Be," he reminded her.

She shrugged. "Okay. That's fine. They can send someone down to Immigration if Angel gets busted. That's all I'm saying."

She waved her hand at the monster. "That's it," she added. "You can go battle that weird thing now."

Doyle took a breath and raised the baseball bat over his head. He yelled, "Chaaarge!" as he dashed toward the creature.

It roared and waggled its hind end at him. Doyle brought down the bat and smacked it hard, bracing himself for impact.

The thing exploded into hundreds of pieces. They were brittle and shiny like fired ceramic, raining down on him like a rain shower. Then they clattered to the floor, rat-a-tatting like buckshot.

For a moment, there was stunned silence throughout the room. Then Celia started jumping up and down and cheering.

"Good job," Father Wahid said.

"Let's move along. *Kris,*" Cordelia said. "Downstairs. Let's look. *Now.*"

Meg opened her eyes. She was confused and disoriented.

Lying on her bed at the Rais compound, she nodded to herself as her memory returned.

I told Jusef I was going to take a nap after our hypnosis session. He had to leave me to lead the sed-hekah.

Something tugged at her mind. She lay quietly, trying to figure out what it was. Nothing came, and she turned over on her side.

She was weary. She felt as if she'd gone jogging.

I have to be careful. The doctor told me overexertion can make the tumor grow, she reminded herself. *And I want to be around for a long, long time.*

Her smile was bittersweet. She was finally standing on the brink of stardom, and she had to be extra careful of her health.

This must be how Naomi Judd felt. Having to quit after they'd struggled so hard to make it to the top.

Well, as Jusef likes to say, Miracles occur every day.

214

She yawned and stretched.

My head hurts, she thought. *It hurts a lot*.

Ignoring the pain, she sat up.

No rest for the weary. We've got a show to do. We'll send old Bang Rais off with a concert that'll snag us a mainstream label.

She smiled and went to take a shower.

Angel woke slowly and painfully. He couldn't figure out where he was, except that it was dark and full of smoke.

He hurt all over. He wasn't sure if he could move. In his weakened condition it would be much harder for him to deal with injuries.

He raised his head. It was pitch dark. The smoke made his eyes water, and his head was spinning.

Inhaling sharply—not out of necessity, just habit—he lifted his head. He groaned.

"S-someone," came a hoarse whisper, followed by a lot of coughing.

"Hello?" he managed.

"I'm . . ." The voice trailed off.

Angel rolled over on his side. He rested a moment. Then he got to his elbows.

"Hello?" the voice called querulously.

"I'm here. Hold on."

The smoke was rising; it seemed a bit thinner as he inched along what must be a cement floor.

Shards of glass punctured the sides of his hands as he made his way across them.

It seemed to take an hour to cover perhaps a foot. Then his hand grazed a pointed, heeled shoe. A woman's shoe.

There was a yelp, almost inhuman. Then the voice rasped, "I thought you died."

"I'm here."

He put his hand gently over her instep. She burst into tears.

"Oh, thank God," she murmured. "So . . . so scared. Cold."

She was in shock, he realized. It was stifling in the room or whatever it was they were in.

"Here's my coat," he told her. Slightly more mobile, he managed to peel it off. It adhered to his upper back and along his triceps, indicating that he was bleeding there.

I must have fallen through a window, he thought. *Or a skylight. The Bonaventure has glass elevators, too. And a revolving restaurant.*

"Here," he said. "I'm draping my coat over you."

"Thank you," she whispered. The woman was weeping. "Please, tell me your name."

"Angel."

"Are you Hispanic?"

"No. Irish, actually."

"You don't sound Irish." Her voice was slightly

stronger but still barely audible. But he was glad she was talking. That was the best way to keep her from panicking. Or becoming unconscious.

"I haven't been home in a long time," he told her.

"I'm from L.A.," she offered. She paused. "It's my wedding anniversary."

"Oh." He didn't know what to say. He wondered what had become of her husband. If he was looking for her in a blind panic. If he'd been hurt in the fire.

Or worse.

"Our fiftieth. Our golden."

"Congratulations," Angel said hoarsely.

"My husband's been dead almost a year." There was a long, shuddering pause. "I'm here alone."

He realized now that the shoe he had touched was beaded. She was all dressed up. With somewhere to go.

But no one to go there with.

"I'm sorry," he said.

"We had no kids." She began to cough again. "No grandkids, of course. He was a professor."

The coughing overtook her. Angel found her shoulders and held onto them, more for comfort than anything else. He couldn't do much else. If she passed out from smoke inhalation, he couldn't give her CPR. He didn't have the lung capacity. Air not an issue.

"We have friends," she murmured. He thought she was rambling. "Many are gone."

He kept hold of her shoulders.

"But I . . ." She took a breath. "I did something."

He closed his eyes. She assumed they were going to die here; she was going to confess her deepest, darkest secret to him.

"I had a baby. I was a young girl." She started crying. "All my life, I've wondered. Boy? Girl?" She lowered her voice. "He was Oriental. It was very frowned upon."

"They wouldn't let you get married," he ventured.

"He loved me. . . ." Her voice trailed off again.

Angel heard the crackling of flames, the roar of fire winds. The fire was getting closer.

"I'm going to explore a little," he said. "Try to find a way out."

"No," she pleaded. "Don't leave me alone." She moved her hand to his as he held on to her shoulder. "Please, young man. I'm so terrified."

He started to object, but something tugged at him, and he said, "All right."

"My child would be all grown up. Every year, I've kept track of how old she would be." She sighed. "I don't know if it's a girl or boy. But I always pictured a girl."

Between coughing spasms, she cried harder. "I don't even know if she knows about me. Back then, people didn't tell children they were adopted. It was such a shameful secret. I never even told my husband that I'd had a baby."

Angel blinked, surprised.

"We were so innocent in those days," she added with a rueful laugh. "He probably thought my little stretch marks were part of a woman's normal appearance. I didn't have many," she added proudly.

"But you never told him."

"I never told him," she whispered. "I never told anyone. My mother sent me away to have the baby. It was what we did in those days. No girlfriends, no sisters, no one knew." Her voice grew faint. "No one ever knew."

"It kept you alone," he said.

"It was my secret," she murmured. "A secret like that, a terrible secret, it sets you apart for life. At first I thought I would forget." Her sorrow cut him as she wept against his hand. "But how could I ever forget?"

"Now I know," he said. "I know, and before I . . . die, I'll tell someone else."

"You understand," she marveled. Again, there was a long silence. Then she said, "How could you, so young, know pain that deep?"

"You did."

"I did." She took a breath. "I'm Roberta Anne Hartford. My maiden name was Anderson. I gave birth to my daughter in Cincinnati, in 1947. I named her Mae. It sounded Chinese." She keened. "I never saw her father again. I don't know what happened to him."

"I'll find out," Angel told her. "Tell me everything you can remember. Everything."

"I've not forgotten a thing," she replied. "I can't remember my driver's license number. Sometimes I have to count back to remember how old I am. But I've never forgotten a thing about him."

She coughed again. "He was eighteen when we met. He was here to become an engineer."

She told her story until it was done. Her voice growing hoarser, fainter, her eyes spilling with tears from the fire and from grief, she told it even as the firefighters started hacking at the walls to save the two of them.

She told it even when her chest, too filled with smoke, began to rise and fall like a hummingbird's.

She told it when the paramedics shown a light in her aged yet beautiful face and announced, "Fully dilated. Sir, we're so sorry."

With the sheet over her still, frail form, she told her story.

Because, as he followed the stretcher out, Angel committed it to memory with every fiber of his being.

CHAPTER ELEVEN

Father Wahid shouted, "This is it!"

It was a silver-and-black sword, wickedly curved. He sliced the air with it.

"So that's a *kris*," Doyle commented, giving it a once-over. "I'm actually a little disappointed. Thought it would look more magickal, somehow."

"Things are not always as they seem," Father Wahid told him.

"I suppose."

"Now I've got to get the Book," he announced. He seemed positively gleeful.

I guess since we've got all the pieces, Cordelia thought, *now we can pass Go and collect the $200.*

"Doyle, you go with him," Cordelia said.

Doyle nodded. "You stay here and take care of the little girl."

"Will do," she said. "Plug in my cell phone in the limo. If Angel calls, let me know."

Doyle nodded. "I will." He turned to Father Wahid. "You've got to tell us where the Book is," he said. "My vision had something to do with Meg Taruma, and she's not here. I need to be able to put the pieces together for Angel."

"Vision?" Father asked neutrally.

"She's in a club." *The T-shirt!* Doyle clapped a hand to his forehead. "Club Komodo." He looked expectantly at the priest. "Please. You've got to tell Cordy so she can tell Angel. It's not like we're going to tell the Raises."

Still, the priest was clearly uncertain. He said, "I've managed this long without sharing it." His hands shook. "You can't know what it's been like, hiding out, wondering if the next sound I hear is death coming for me." He coughed into his hand. "And I've been ill."

He's kind of whining, Cordelia thought, mildly annoyed. *We've just reached true yay and I, at least, am giddy and up. As Buffy used to say.*

She smiled to herself. *Wow, we're doing as well as the Slayer, just about. Except for stopping the bad guy from either taking over or destroying the world.*

In our case, destroying seems more likely.

"Didn't you say the stars align tonight?" Doyle pressed. "Isn't this the most powerful night and like that?"

The man sighed. His shoulders slumped. "No, you're right. If something happens to me, someone will have to complete the work."

His voice dropped to a whispered, "There's a warehouse. A sweatshop. A hellish place. Some of my parishoners work there, hoping one day to pay off their passage and enjoy the great life they believed was waiting for them here. I hid the Book in a copy of *English as a Second Language.*"

"Yeah, a few innocent people died because the Raises were searching for the copy with the Book sewn into it," Doyle commented. "Not that we're blaming you," he added quickly.

"Right," Cordelia assured him. "Because we understand that sometimes people die even if they're not directly involved."

"So. The sweatshop," Doyle said.

"The actual Book of Latura is in that warehouse. It's on Seventh." Father Wahid gave the street number.

"Close to Fashion Alley," Cordelia said knowledgeably.

"Thank you, Father," Doyle said.

"I pray to God I haven't signed our death warrants," Father Wahid murmured.

"Better ours than the world's." Doyle smiled wanly. He turned to Cordelia. "Tell Angel to check out Club Komodo. It may be a fancy name for Hell."

She swallowed. "Witness my surprise."

❖   ❖   ❖

In his refrigerator Angel had a container of chilled pig's blood, three pieces of bread, and one piece of cheddar cheese. Her stomach growling, Cordy made Celia a sandwich. As Celia wolfed it down, Cordy nibbled on the extra piece of bread.

The good news is, I've probably lost weight, she thought. *The bad news is, if we all die, I'll waste away to nothing.*

Celia sat down to watch TV, and Cordelia paced.

Just about the time she couldn't take the tension any more, the phone finally rang.

"It's me," Angel said.

"Oh, Angel! Oh, thank god!"

"We don't have time for pleasantries," Angel said. "Do you have anything for me?"

"There's something about a Club Komodo. Doyle didn't know where it is. But it was part of his vision."

"Then I'll find it," Angel said.

"Wait!"

But Angel had already hung up.

Angel snagged a ride from one of the paramedics who had rescued him. She was going off duty, and she assured him that Santa Monica was on her way. It was like that in Los Angeles: An hour or more commute to work was not unusual.

She was an extremely cut Texan with long, straight black hair, and she passed the drive time alternately flirting with Angel and describing in vivid detail the grossest accidents she had worked on.

"Motorcycles are the worst, definitely," she said, making a left against oncoming traffic. Horns blared and she cheerfully flipped someone off.

She's a worse driver than Cordelia, if that's possible, he thought, bracing for impact. *Also, ruder.*

"We call 'em donor cycles." Her smile was ghoulish. "No, but wait." She nodded. "The worst are these burn victims we've been getting. I don't know what the hell's going on with those, but they're worse than the cycles."

Bingo, Angel thought. He said carefully, "Burn victims?"

"It's gangs. Gotta be," she said authoritatively.

The moon shone on the black water. Angel remembered his dream about Buffy and felt a tug. Back in Sunnydale, the mayor—himself an aspiring demon—had blamed most of the supernatural occurrences in Sunnydale on "gangs on PCP." It was ludicrous, but the good people of the little town on the hellmouth had hidden their heads in the sand and accepted the explanation.

Angelenos were only slightly more capable of accepting the truth about the dark side.

"Why do you say that?" he asked. "Why gangs?"

"Well, I'm not a cop." She sounded a little guarded. "But it's always gangs these days." Shrugging, she added, "New people come in, try to steal territory, everyone gets pissed off."

"And kill civilians?"

She scrutinized him. "Funny, I didn't notice any bruises on your butt."

"Excuse me?"

"From when you fell out of the turnip truck. You cannot be this ignorant and live."

"I've been out of the loop," he ventured.

"What loop? This is not a loop. This is life. Common sense."

"How are they different from other burn victims?" he asked, trying another tack.

She went with it. "Burned from the inside out. Our guess is they're forced to swallow some kind of combustible material. The material must be timed to go off inside 'em. There's gotta be some kind of oxygen source, too, to get it started and/or keep it going. Then, ka-blam. Y'all got yourself a kinda flare-gun effect going on in there."

She shrugged. "Me, I'd like to go in my sleep. Or having sex." She grinned at him. "Don't they call it 'the little death' for a reason?"

Before he could answer, she said, "There was a movie with Madonna, wasn't there? She killed guys on purpose by sleeping with them? I'm sorry, but that's just dang ridiculous. Not to mention extremely egotistical. Shee-*oot*." She winked at him.

"I'm off-duty, but I still talk like a lady. That's all I do like a lady, though."

She merged into the right lane, barely missing a Mercedes. The other driver slammed on the horn.

"I'm a bodybuilder. I supposed I could kill some guy I was sleepin' with, if I wanted to." She gave him another look. "And I guess sometimes a girl wants to, if he's been a pig. Some men change once they get what they want."

"Mmmm." *Sex and bitter consequences.* The conversation was hitting a little close to home. "How many have there been? Deaths, I mean?"

"At least a dozen." She made a face. "They reek."

They do. Death smells bad.

He nodded politely. Then he gestured through the windshield and said, "Brake lights on."

"I see 'em." His companion sighed as she didn't slow one single mile. "It's true what they say in this town. All the good ones are gay or married."

He looked at her curiously.

She laughed. "Well, hell, I sure don't think you're gay. But there's no temptation in your eyes, and you and I both know it wouldn't kill you to do the nasty with me tonight. Which is as much as any lady ought to say."

He made no answer.

She brayed like a truck driver. "The men out here

are sure not cowboys. Hell, this keeps up, I'm moving back to Dallas."

Near the pier, she screamed over to a hotel parking lot. She dropped him off and gave him a friendly wave. "You ever get in a life-threatening accident again, ask for Jessie," she said. "I'll take good care of you. Nobody can intubate better than me." She wrinkled her nose. "Just ask my last two boyfriends."

Angel smiled. "Thanks."

"Take care. There's a bottle of George Dickel and some Dwight Yoakum at my house, you change your mind. And Dwight, well, let's just say he works for me. By the way, I wrote my phone number on your underwear while the doc was examining you."

"Another time," he said gently.

"Oh, yeah, right. By the way, I also have a shower." She gave him a smile. "You don't stink. You just smell like smoke."

He was at the pier, and it was still jumping. In the distance, he saw the silhouette of a concrete building lined in neon. It said "Club Komodo." He headed for it, then stood gazing at the sign as someone stood on the balcony below it, preparing to jump.

"Meg, no!" Angel cried.

She blinked. Frowned. She said, "Who?"

Her face changed. Over it, he saw the hideous mask he once had seen in the dusky barn, the night he and Dorrie had gone to Granny Quinn's.

She—or it, whatever it was—stared at him and said, "Evil has a long memory, Angelus. Evil can bear grudges. It can hate. It can plot its revenge.

"But good? Good must forgive. It must forget.

"That's why you'll be forgotten. The evil inside you will cancel out your pathetic attempts to make amends. How can you ever hope to walk with the true angels? You're a mass murderer. You belong with us."

He stared, not understanding. "Are you Meg Taruma?" he asked, trying to move forward.

She shrugged. "One name's as good as another. But no matter what you call me, I'll be back. Because evil is eternal.

"That's the truth of immortality."

Then she dived off the building and landed on her back on the pavement.

In Angel's apartment a blue figure shimmered into being. He was tall for an Indonesian. Muscular and robust, he had a square chin and a hooked nose.

He was Bang Rais, ascendant. He had dared to shed his mortal body, risking everything to gain life eternal. Did Jusef not remember that Latura would grant immortality to one person and one only? Did he think the god would turn his back on his most devoted Servant because of the desires of an impatient young man?

I have killed more people for Latura than you can imagine, Bang Rais thought. *There are entire villages gone. Ethnic populations.*

But more important, I have persuaded other people to kill for Latura on my behalf, by letting them think they would take my place. My son tortured dozens. He learned the secret of burning their hearts, and thought he could usurp my place.

But I kept him busy. I kept him wondering. I killed people and I moved their bodies. I planted many false clues. He looked around and headed for the kitchen. *And all the while, I deflected attention from the truth. For behold:*

In his office in Club Komodo, Jusef picked up the phone and said, "Start the fires."

All over Los Angeles, other phones were dialed, and picked up.

Gas cans were dumped over. Matches struck. One by one, fires erupted and blazed.

And the people screamed. Immigrant men and women, locked behind doors so that they wouldn't take breaks. Children, overcome by smoke.

Sirens shrieked down the traffic corridors of Los Angeles. The city filled with smoke. The death toll rose. And rose.

And rose.

*   *   *

It's time, Jusef thought. He put his guitar strap over his head and went onstage. The band was waiting.

"Meg?" he called.

When she didn't appear, he looked at the audience, patiently waiting, and ran his fingertips over the strings.

The gamelan musicians began to run their hammers and cymbals up and down the scales. The exotic, ancient music of Indonesia filled the room.

With a flourish, Slamet walked onstage. He held against his chest a small pile of bamboo rods.

They were the original writings of the First Servant's daughter, preserved all this time by the good fathers of the Nias church.

From them, Jusef had learned that a *pustaha lakek* had been written, and another would be dictated by the god through the drums of his people, the headhunters of Nias. It would contain misinformation.

It would prevent the one who used it from achieving his immortality.

He had known all this, but he had let his father think that he, Bang Rais, had the upper hand. Jusef had caused his death on purpose. He had pretended to hunt for the Book, concocting the silly scheme about *English as a Second Language* because he, Jusef, remembered the book with hatred from his days in school.

He had known very well that this was Latura's

special night, when the dark powers were the most concentrated.

"Meg?" he called again.

Bang Rais, in his more evolved form, smiled at the vessel which would bring Latura into the world. From reading the Book of Latura, he had known what to look for.

It hadn't been Meg.

And she hadn't possessed any special blood.

He had made that all up, the better to entrap and distract his son and, if need be, his nephew.

I fooled them all, he thought. *In the end, I'm the one who will be immortal.*

"Celia, Angel has one can of Sprite," Cordelia said as she walked from the refrigerator. "Do you want it?"

There was no answer.

"Celia?"

Cordelia turned around and saw him.

She dropped the can on Angel's carpet.

He only said, "It's too late."

Then he disappeared, taking Celia with him.

As Angel held Meg Taruma in his arms, his cell phone rang.

"Angel, this blue guy just took Celia and I'll bet they're going to where the Book is," she babbled.

"Slow down."

"The vessel was Celia Sucharitkul," she said. "Not Meg. Someone lied to someone else."

"Give me the address," he said.

She did so.

"I'm going there now," she added.

Angel held Meg. He didn't know precisely what she was now, or what had happened to her, but he had been connected to her. Inside, she had been sweet and frightened, vulnerable and desperately in need of help.

Then, as she began to die, he saw her lifetime unfold:

She'd been an unremarkable young woman living in an unremarkable part of Dakarta. The most exciting part of her day was spent feeding her cat, whose name she didn't remember.

She had never been to Nias. All that was a dream. A lie.

She opened her eyes and looked up at him.

"The injections," she said. "They made me dream an entire life."

It had been some kind of drug to stimulate her mind. To make the false memories more real.

"But we connected," she whispered to him.

"We did," he answered.

But had they? Had he actually been bitten by a serpent?

That way lies madness, he told himself.

As she died, Meg began to cry.

"It wasn't me," she said. "I don't know who I am. I'm going to die and I won't ever know who I was."

Angel held her. When she faded away, he looked into her cold, blank eyes.

He didn't know who she was, either.

The place where the sweatshop was located was grubbier and dirtier than the rest of the garment district. It also wasn't far from where Celia had snatched Cordelia's purse.

Doyle followed the priest up two flights of stairs. He pushed open a door and stared in dismay and disgust at the filth and stench of a room filled with sewing machines. A teddy bear lay under one of them; under another, a small stack of children's books. Father Wahid stopped to sort through it.

This is where they kept the little ones. Forced them to work.

The room was dark and dingy. Doyle crossed deeper into it and found a flight of stairs that only went down. *Talk about a mystery house.*

He took them.

What he saw made his stomach clench.

It was a terrible place. Paintings of tortures and different kinds of executions were streaked across the walls. From the ceiling hung skulls and bones. In the center, bodies which had just begun to rot.

In the middle of the room was a large stone table.

And tied to the table, little Celia.

"The vessel," said a voice.

It was Father Wahid.

He was dressed in a black robe, and as Doyle stared, leathery wings beat overhead.

Two repulsive flying monsters with crackled green skin, each the size of a lion, flapped their wings overhead. Each carried a round object in its mouth.

As one, they released the objects, and they splatted against the filthy floor.

They were human heads.

Slamet's, and Jusef's.

Father Wahid threw back his head and laughed. "They thought they were so clever," he said. "They lied and cheated so much that they couldn't remember if they'd lied to each other. In the end, they lied to themselves.

"I am the real Servant. I'm the one who'll become immortal."

Doyle shrugged. "I don't really care," he said.

Then he lunged at the erstwhile priest with the sword.

Angel let the coroner take Meg away. Then he set about hailing a cab to get to the address Cordelia had given him.

As one pulled up, he sat for a moment. Then he

said, "Rais Compound. It's up in the hills. I'll give you directions."

The cabbie was attentive. They made good time.

But as Angel glanced through the window, he realized that day was close at hand.

In fact, he wasn't sure he had enough time to get to the compound.

Doesn't matter, he thought.

The cabbie chatted incessantly. Angel didn't really listen. He was reviewing his life.

Because this may very well be the end of it.

What had he been promised? That he would die alone, and forgotten?

"We're here," the cabbie told him. "I don't think they'll let me through the gates."

"That's okay."

Angel got out and gave the man enough money to make him go away. Then he turned to the guard, said "Hey," and slammed his fist into the man's jaw. The guard crumpled.

Another shouted "Stop!" and aimed a weapon directly at Angel.

Angel picked up speed and slid on his hands, like a batter stealing a base. The man, startled, shot high.

Pushing him off his feet, Angel darted past.

Gunfire pursued him as he took the temple stairs two, three, four at a time. He didn't so much descend as fall.

There was a single torch flickering in the blackness of the temple.

The statue of Latura had grown to an enormous size, and it was batting at a thick horde of flying *jin*, plucking them and tossing them into its mouth.

"Granny Quinn," Angel called out.

The statue stopped moving. It swiveled its ugly stone head toward him. Fires burned in the eyes.

"Granny Quinn," he said again.

"That's not my name." The voice was loud enough to hollow out more caverns. The fires in the eyes were so hot that blisters formed on Angel's face and arms.

"Evil's your name," Angel said. "Isn't it?"

"If you like."

The statue made a fist and slammed it down beside Angel. "And what is yours? Crown Prince of Nothing?"

"It was all for me, wasn't it?" Angel demanded, advancing. "Like an experiment, to see which way I'd go. Because part of me is evil—"

"Very evil," the statue said, showing huge fangs as it grinned at him.

"And part of me is good."

It was difficult for Angel to say. So he said it again.

"Part of me is good."

The statue laughed. "Everyone's got darkness and light."

"Not like me. I'm unique. That's what makes me the perfect vessel."

"Interesting," the statue said.

"And that's what you miss. Feeling interested. That much of the story of Latura is true. Death's limited. And life—for most people—is transitory.

"Which makes it seem pointless."

The statue lowered its face. "So say you."

"Around me, everyone lives and dies. They make choices for lightness or darkness. I'm the only one who keeps living, and who keeps struggling.

"It's I who am the God of Death. I'm the one who rose from the Underworld to walk among people for an eternity."

"Such pride." The statue mockingly shook its finger.

"You're simply a demon. A clever, bored demon," Angel said.

The huge stone figure inclined its head. "Golgothla is my name, vampire. And you're right. It's you I want. Not the Servant. Not the Vessel. Doreen. Alice. Meg. Hendrik. Wahid. Bang. You are unique."

It shrugged. "But now that you know, the game is over. It's no longer interesting. If I let you escape, sooner or later you'll find a way to destroy me."

The creature made a fist and slammed it into Angel. Then it kicked, sending the vampire flying across the cavern. Angel crashed into the rock wall and ricocheted onto his back.

He was so stunned he could see nothing but blackness. The floor shook as the demon statue came toward him. Its laughter loosened rock from the ceiling. It clattered down on Angel's head and chest, bruising and battering him.

Moving like a slow-motion dream, Angel rolled over. After a few seconds he pressed forward on his hands and thrust backward onto his feet. He assumed a classic kickboxing defensive position, and waited for his attacker to make another move.

Then he realized what the game was: He could not die. His life had been given back to him by the Powers That Be, and it was not his to dispose of.

That was what made him interesting. He had something to lose, and his stakes were high.

So what do I do, fight until I drop? Until I die? Until it gets tired of me?

"It's no different from oblivion for you, is it?" Angel said. "The outcome of this doesn't really matter."

"Of course it does. It matters if you destroy me," it whispered in a tantalizing voice.

"To you? Doubtful," Angel said. "You have no real self. If you die in this form, you'll rise again in another. Evil is eternal."

"How cynical," said the demon. "Makes you want to give up, doesn't it?"

"No." Angel raised his chin. "It makes me want to live forever, too."

Then he came at the demon, landing punches everywhere. Its flying minions harried Angel, biting his face and head, aiming for the nape of his neck.

The floor exploded and nightmare creatures gushed out like a lava river. Angel fought so many they became a blur.

"Tired yet?" he flung at the monster. "Bored yet? You don't want to kill me, do you. Because I'm the best the good side's got down here."

"Enough!" the demon shouted.

Then it burst apart into hundreds of pieces.

Each piece became a face, but each face was the same. They all shrieked with frustration.

Then those pieces exploded.

And those pieces.

And those.

Until Angel lay, exhausted, in a field of sand.

EPILOGUE

"You're forgiven, not forgotten."
—The Corrs

Éire Shaor was a strange and wonderful place: an authentic Irish working-class bar located smack in the middle of West Hollywood. How Doyle had found it, Angel had no idea, but he was pleasantly surprised by the half-demon's discovery.

Reading Angel's expression, Doyle said, "This beats a deserted library, eh?"

Doyle and Angel sat within view of the dartboard, each drinking a pint, each quietly watching the game. Angel listened to the Irish groups on the sound system: the Chieftains, the Corrs, Clannad. Harp music. A romanticized Ireland, to be sure.

Cordelia might have liked it, but she was on a date with Jason the policeman.

"Were you ever in the IRA?" Doyle asked as he picked up his glass beer mug and drank. "Sinn Fein and all that?" He gestured to the name of the bar, which translated as "Free Ireland."

Angel looked at him curiously. "Why do you ask?"

"Remember when they wouldn't let Gerry Adams into the States? And them with all those Irish Kennedys and such?"

"Them?"

"The Americans." Doyle frowned. "What did you think I meant, the *humans?*"

Angel said nothing.

"Don't forget, I'm half-human."

"No way I can."

Doyle appeared content to let that one go. They sat in silence for a while. Then Doyle said, "I get homesick, y'know." He made little circles on the bar with the bottom of his mug. "Oh, I do okay here, but back home, it's a bit easier to get by."

"To pass," Angel teased, "for human."

"Well, then, you're a bitter boyo." Doyle regarded him. "You'd be as much out of place in Ireland these days as you are here. No matter where you go, you're a stranger in a strange land."

Angel looked at him. "It's not a strange land."

Doyle snorted. "Los Angeles? Go on. It's the most bizarre place on earth."

"Not by half," Angel insisted.

"They're tofu-eating sun-worshippers. Nothing is organized to suit you. Nothing is convenient for you."

Angel said nothing.

"Beside which, it must be like walking through a minefield every day, seeing people together, oblivious of the horrors. Building lives, making plans."

Angel looked at him.

"Able to make love to one another without worrying about going to hell. The ones who aren't Catholic, anyway."

"Doyle," Angel said tiredly.

"Well, it's nice to know you admit it. A vampire with a soul . . ." He shrugged. "You're an odd duck."

Angel lifted his beer.

"Yes," he said. "For a while, anyway."

Maybe forever.

"To Ireland," Angel said.

Doyle smiled faintly and raised his glass.

About the Author

Bestselling author Nancy Holder has sold 42 novels and 200 short stories. She has received four Bram Stoker awards for fiction from the Horror Writers Association. Writing with her frequent collaborator, Christopher Golden, as well as working alone, she has sold fifteen *Buffy the Vampire Slayer* and *Angel* projects. Her most recent Buffy project, *The Watcher's Guide, Vol. 2*, written with the assistance of Jeff Mariotte and Maryelizabeth Hart, will be out this fall.

Buffy the Vampire Slayer™

"Well, we could grind our enemies into powder with a sledgehammer, but gosh, we did that last night."

—Xander

As long as there have been vampires, there has been the Slayer. One girl in all the world, to find them where they gather and to stop the spread of their evil...the swell of their numbers.

LOOK FOR A NEW TITLE EVERY MONTH!

Based on the hit TV series created by
Joss Whedon

2400

. . . A GIRL BORN
WITHOUT THE FEAR GENE

FEARLESS™

A NEW SERIES BY
FRANCINE PASCAL

A TITLE AVAILABLE EVERY MONTH

From Pocket Pulse
Published by Pocket Books